ALSO BY ELIZABETH EULBERG

The Lonely Hearts Club

Prom & Prejudice

Take a Bow

Revenge of the Girl with the Great Personality

We Can Work It Out

ELIZABETH EULBERG

Better
off
Friends

Point

Copyright © 2014 by Elizabeth Eulberg

This book was originally published in hardcover by Point in 2014.

All rights reserved. Published by Point, an imprint of Scholastic Inc., *Publishers since 1920*. SCHOLASTIC, POINT, and associated logos are trademarks and/or registered trademarks of Scholastic Inc.

The publisher does not have any control over and does not assume any responsibility for author or third-party websites or their content.

ISBN 978-0-545-87211-9

10 9 8 7 6 5 4 3   17 18 19

Printed in the U.S.A.   40
First printing 2015

The text type was set in New Century Schoolbook.
Book design by Elizabeth B. Parisi

For Erin Black, Sheila Marie Everett,

and Elizabeth Parisi

because this author is better off

having you in her corner

Guys and girls can be friends.

Way to get right to the point, Levi.

All I'm saying is that it's possible for guys and girls to be friends. I've never understood what the big deal is. I mean, yeah, we've had to deal with all those stupid questions.

Oh, the questions.

Are you guys together?

Why not?

You've hooked up at some point, right?

Or thought of it?

Macallan, how could you resist Levi's considerable charms?

That has never happened.

I don't know. . . .

Well, I do. And it's never happened. Ever.

Okay, fine. But I'll admit it hasn't been totally easy. We've had some problems.

Some problems?

All right, more than a few. But look how everything turned out. I don't think either of us thought we'd even speak to each other again after my first day at school, back in seventh grade. Especially since you must've had a huge crush on me.

Are you remembering the same day that I am?

Yes.

Oh. I'm so sorry. I believe you're suffering from delusional fantasies.

I'm not delusional. There are many words to describe me: *awesome*, *stud*, *male extraordinaire*, you name it.

Fine. You're awesome. But clearly delusional.

CHAPTER ONE

I was probably the first kid ever excited for summer to be over. There was too much free time that summer, which can lead to too much thinking, especially for a loss-stricken eleven-year-old. I couldn't wait for seventh grade to start. To dive into schoolwork. To distract myself from the loneliest facts. At one point, I regretted turning down Dad's offer to spend the summer in Ireland with Mom's family. But I knew that if I went, there would be reminders of her everywhere. Not like there wasn't one every time I looked in the mirror.

So the only escape I had was school. When I got the message that I was to report to the main office before class, I was worried I'd be faced with another year of forced visits with the school counselor, looks of pity from my fellow classmates, and well-meaning but oblivious faculty members who kept telling me it was "important to keep her memory alive."

Like I could ever forget her.

I wasn't ready for any additional drama that morning. It was already the first day of a new school year *since*.

"Do you want me to go with you, Macallan?" Emily asked after I received my summons to the office. A tight smile on her face gave away the concern she thought she was hiding.

"No, it's okay," I replied. "I'm sure it's nothing."

She studied me for a second before adjusting my hair clip. "Well, if you need me, I'll be in Mr. Nelson's class."

I gave her a reassuring smile and kept it on my face as I entered the office.

Principal Blaska greeted me with a hug. "Welcome back, Macallan! How was your summer?"

"Great!" I lied.

We both stared at each other, neither knowing what to say next.

"Well, I'm going to need your assistance today with a new student. Meet Levi Rodgers — he's from Los Angeles!"

I looked over and saw this boy with long blond hair pulled into a low ponytail. His hair was even longer than mine. He tucked a loose strand behind his ear before he reached out his hand and said, "Hey."

I had to give him credit — at least he had manners . . . for a surfer dude.

Principal Blaska handed me his schedule. "Could you show him around and take him to his first class?"

"Of course."

I led Levi out into the hallway and started giving him the five-cent tour. I wasn't in the mood to play *What's Your Life Story?*

"The building is basically in the shape of a T. Down this hallway you have your math, science, and history classes." I started motioning my arms like a flight attendant. "Then behind you, English and language classes as well as study hall." I started walking fast. "And there's the gym, cafeteria, and music and art rooms. Oh, and there are bathrooms at the end of each hall as well as a bubbler."

His eyebrows shot up. "What's a bubbler?"

My immediate reaction was one of disbelief. How could he not know what a bubbler is?

"Um, where you can get water. To drink." I walked him over to it and turned the handle for the water to come out of the spout.

"Oh, you mean a *water fountain*."

"Yes. Water fountain, bubbler — whatever."

He laughed. "I've never heard it called a bubbler before."

My response was to walk faster.

As his eyes swept the hallway, I noticed they were light blue, almost gray. "It's so weird," he went on. "You could fit this entire school in my old school's cafeteria." His voice went up at the end of everything he said, like it was a question. "It's, like, going to be a lot to adjust to, ya know?"

I knew this was supposed to be the point where I politely asked him about his old school, but I wanted to get to class as soon as possible.

A few friends passed by to say hello, everyone checking out the new guy. Our school was fairly small; the majority of us had been together since fifth grade, if not kindergarten.

I stole another glance at him. It was hard to decipher if he was cute. His hair was practically white in places, probably from the sun. His tan made his light hair and pale eyes stick out even more — but this wouldn't be for very long, since in Wisconsin we rarely see the sun past August.

Levi had on a checkered button-down paired with long cargo shorts and flip-flops. It was as if he couldn't decide whether to dress up or be casual. I luckily had Emily to help me pick out my first-day-of-school outfit that day: a bright-yellow-and-white-striped sundress with a white cardigan.

Levi gave me an eager smile. "So what kind of name is Macallan? Or is it McKayla?"

My initial instinct was to ask him if the name Levi came from the jeans his mom was wearing on the day he was born, but instead I behaved like the good, responsible student I was supposed to be.

"It's a family name," I said. Which wasn't a total lie — it was someone's family name, just not mine. While I loved that I had a unique name, it was always a little embarrassing to admit it was because my dad liked a certain kind of Scotch whiskey. "It's Ma-*cal*-lan."

"Dude, that's cool."

I couldn't believe he'd just called me *dude*.

"Yeah, thanks." I finished the tour at his first class, English. "Well, here you are."

He looked at me expectantly, like I was supposed to find him a desk and tuck him in good night.

"Hi, Macallan!" Mr. Driver greeted me. "I didn't think I had you until later today. Oh, wait, you must be Levi."

"Yes, I'm showing him around. Well" — I turned to Levi — "I've got to catch class. Good luck."

"Oh, okay," he stammered. "See ya around?"

It was at that moment I realized the look he had was fear. He was scared. Of course he was. I felt a pang of guilt but quickly shook it off as I walked to my first class.

I had enough problems as it was.

Emily got down to business the second we were in line at lunch that day.

"So what's the deal with the new guy?" she asked.

I shrugged my shoulders. "I don't know. He's okay."

She examined a slice of pizza. "His hair is *so* long."

"He's from California," I offered.

"What else do you know about him?" She discarded the pizza and picked up a chicken sandwich and salad. I followed suit.

I was so thankful that I had a girly-girl friend like Emily. My dad, as much as he tried, couldn't really help me out with things like hair, clothes, and makeup. If left to his own devices, I'd wear jeans, sneakers, and a Green Bay Packers T-shirt every day, and eat pizza for every meal. And Emily was as girly as you could get. She was easily one of the prettiest girls in our class, with long, shiny jet-black hair, and dark brown eyes. She also had the best clothes, and I was so glad we were the same size so I could borrow them, although she was already way more developed than I was. At least I would have someone to go to once I needed a bra. I couldn't even imagine how awkward that would be for Dad. For both of us.

"Um . . ." I tried to think about what else I learned about Levi. Now, too late, I felt I should've made more of an effort.

Danielle joined us, her honey-colored curls bouncing along

as we walked into the cafeteria. "Is that the new guy?" She pointed to Levi, who was sitting by himself.

"He's so skinny," Emily remarked.

Danielle laughed. "I know, right? But don't worry, if the ButterBurgers don't fatten him up, the cheese curds and brats will."

The three of us started walking to our regular table. Levi's gaze followed us. We were used to this. Usually people liked to make little comments like "a blonde, a redhead, and an Asian walked into a . . ." But I always saw us as "the one you want to sit next to because she's hilarious, the one you want to cheat off of in class, and the one all the guys have a crush on."

I gave Levi a quick smile, hoping to undo some of the rudeness from the morning. He returned with a sad wave. I paused for a second, and in that second, I noticed the look of gratitude on Levi's face. He was expecting me to sit with him or at least invite him over. I hesitated, unsure what to do. I didn't want to play babysitter, but I also knew what it was like to be alone. And scared.

"Guys, I feel bad. Can he sit with us?"

When nobody argued, I approached Levi.

"Hey there — how was your morning?" I asked, trying to smile and be welcoming for a change.

"It was good." The tone in his voice indicated that it was anything but good.

"Do you want to sit with us?" I gestured to our table.

"Thanks." He exhaled deeply.

Soon the attention turned toward gossip of the *I Really Know How You Spent Your Summer Vacation* kind.

Levi sat next to me and picked at his lunch uncomfortably. He put his backpack on the table and I noticed a button pinned onto it.

"That's not —" I stopped myself. What were the chances it was what I thought it was? It'd be way too random.

Levi noticed I was looking at the KEEP CALM AND BLIMEY ON button on his bag. "Oh, there's this totally rad BBC show —" he started to explain.

I could barely contain my excitement. *"Buggy and Floyd.* I love that show!"

His face lit up. "No way — nobody knows *Buggy and Floyd.* This is insane!"

It *was* insane.

Buggy and Floyd followed the zany antics of Theodore "Buggy" Bugsy and his cousin/roommate Floyd. In pretty much every episode, Buggy got himself into some ludicrous trouble that Floyd had to rescue him from. And Floyd was always complaining about the situation, Buggy, and pretty much everything about society.

I felt a smile start to spread across my lips. "Yeah, my mom's family lives in Ireland and I saw it when I visited them a couple summers ago. I have the DVDs at home."

"Me too! My buddy's dad is head of development for a production company and he was thinking about adapting it for here."

I groaned. I hated it when a perfectly awesome show from the UK got changed for the US. Sometimes British humor did not translate and it would end up dumbed down.

"They'd totally ruin it," Levi and I said in unison. Both of us were surprised for a second before we started laughing.

"Favorite episode?" He was leaning forward, his shoulders no longer up toward his ears.

"Oh, there are so many. The one where Floyd's sister is about to give birth —"

"Blimey if I know where to get boiling water unless a cuppa tea counts." Levi's cockney accent was spot-on.

"Yes!" I slammed my hand against the tabletop.

"What's going on over there?" Emily looked inquisitively at both of us.

"You know that British show I've tried to get you to watch?"

"*That?*" Emily shook her head at me like she always did when she found my little eccentricities amusing. She turned toward Levi. "You know about *that*?"

He laughed. "Yeah, it's *so* funny."

"Uh-huh." Emily wrinkled her nose. "It's *adorable* that you have that in common."

"Common!" Levi crowed. "I know I ain't the queen o' England, but I ain't *common*."

This was another line from the show.

"A common nuisance, you are!" we both finished.

Emily looked at us like were aliens. Danielle seemed amused.

We talked a little more about our summers, and when it was time to go, I made sure Levi knew where he was going next. This time when he said, "See ya later," I found myself not dreading the idea. It was pretty cool to have someone around here who didn't like the same things as everybody else.

Emily laughed as we put our trays on the conveyer belt. "So you and your new boyfriend seem to have a lot to talk about."

"Stop it! You know he's not my boyfriend."

"*I* know that, but everybody else in the cafeteria seemed to notice your little lovefest."

She was probably right. People were most likely making comments about our overanimated conversation. But I really didn't care. It would be a welcome change from everything else people had whispered behind my back over the past year.

Uncle Adam was waiting for me after school to take me home. He was always excited to see me, even if he'd dropped me off only a few hours ago.

"How was your first day?" he asked while his arms wrapped tightly around me.

"Good!" I reassured him.

"All right." He grabbed my backpack and started walking me to his car.

Levi was getting into an SUV with a woman I assumed was his mom. He said something to her and she started to walk over to us. With some reluctance, he followed. A knot began to form tightly in my stomach. I always got defensive whenever anybody met Adam for the first time.

Uncle Adam is an amazing person and everybody in town loves him. He's friendly, outgoing, always willing to lend a hand. But he was born with a speech deformity, so when he talks, his speech sounds a little slurred. I'm not exactly sure what it's called, but the back of his throat doesn't close properly, so it can be difficult to understand him sometimes.

When I was little and I asked what was wrong with Uncle Adam, Mom made it clear that there was nothing "wrong" with him, he spoke differently because of a birth defect. So I took it at face value. Then, two years ago, I was walking home from the park when these boys started asking how my "retard uncle" was doing. I yelled, "He's not retarded, he just talks funny." I came home in tears and told my dad what had happened. That's when he informed me that Adam was developmentally disabled. My parents thought I already knew. But what did I know? He drives, has a job, and lives in his own house (right across the street from ours). His life isn't really that different from ours.

I held my breath as she introduced herself to Adam and me, worried that, like some other people, she'd do something wrong. "Hi, Macallan, I'm Levi's mother. Thank you so much for being welcoming to Levi today. It's hard to move halfway across the country and start fresh at a new school." She had the same long blond hair as Levi, but hers was pulled back into a high ponytail. She had on yoga pants and a hoodie. It looked like she was coming back from the gym. Even without makeup on, she was absolutely gorgeous.

"*Mom*," Levi groaned, no doubt trying to prevent her from telling his whole life story.

She turned toward Adam. "And you must be her father."

Uncle Adam grabbed her hand, and I saw her flinch slightly at his grip. "Uncle."

"This is my uncle Adam," I said.

"Very nice to meet you." She gave him a warm smile as he and Levi shook hands, too. I tried to find some hesitation on Levi's part, but it wasn't there. He was probably more focused on getting his mom back to the car.

I found myself nervously overexplaining. "Yeah, my dad sometimes has to work late even though he owns his own construction company, so sometimes Adam leaves the hardware store to take me home."

"Well, if you ever need us to take you home or stay with us until your dad or uncle is done, we'd be more than happy to have you."

I stood there silently for a few seconds. I was used to Midwestern politeness, but here was a woman who'd just moved to town and I'd just met, and she was already offering her home to me. And she was doing it out of niceness, not because she knew about the accident.

"Great! Wednesdays are always hard," Uncle Adam said before I could stop him. He usually worked from seven in the morning until two, so he could pick me up from school. Except on Wednesdays, when he had the late shift. Last year, I either stayed in the library or got a ride with Emily or Danielle after their respective after-school activities.

Levi's mom didn't hesitate. "Why don't you come over on Wednesday? Only if you want."

I glanced over at Levi, who looked at me and mouthed the words she'd just said — *only if you want*.

"Sure!" Uncle Adam agreed.

"I'll give you my number, and Macallan's father can call me if he has any concerns, okay?"

Levi pointed to the button on his bag, his eyebrow arching in a playful manner. I imagined us watching *Buggy and Floyd* together.

I do, I mouthed back.

The two adults exchanged phone numbers. The negative me said Levi's mom was doing this because she thought my uncle was unfit to look after me. The positive me said she was a nice person who wanted her son to have friends.

Or maybe she feels sorry for you, the negative me said.

She doesn't know, the positive me spoke up. This wasn't the same thing as a non-friend suddenly paying attention to you or offering a shoulder to cry on, or bringing over a casserole that was nothing your mother would have ever, ever cooked for you.

Uncle Adam and I got into his car. He always made sure I was buckled up properly before he turned on the ignition.

"Everything okay?" He looked at me intently.

"Yeah," I said, even though I had no idea how to feel about what had just happened. I didn't really like unexpected turns. I'd had more than my share by that point.

Adam looked so sad. "Your mother loved picking you up from school."

I nodded, which was pretty much the only response I had whenever anybody brought her up.

A tear started trickling down his face. "You look so much like her."

I'd been getting used to this. I loved that I looked like my mother. I had her big hazel eyes, heart-shaped face, and wavy auburn hair that turned strawberry blond in the summer.

But I was also that mirror girl, the walking reminder of what we all had lost.

I closed my eyes, took a deep breath, and promised myself: *In fifteen minutes, you can work on algebra homework. In fifteen minutes, you'll have a reprieve. Get through these next fifteen minutes and you'll be fine.*

Do you really think my mom offered to give you a ride out of pity?

Not anymore. Now I know your mom is the definition of incredible.

Like mother, like son.

Oh, please.

But you admit you only invited me to sit with you at lunch out of pity.

Totally.

See, you're supposed to lie and say you wanted to hang out with me because you thought I was beyond cool.

So you want me to lie?

Um, *yeah*. Friends lie to make each other feel better. You didn't know that?

Have I told you that you look really cute today?

Thanks, I — *Wait a second.*

CHAPTER TWO

I was upset when my parents first told me we were moving to Wisconsin. Like, why did I have to totally give up my friends and my life because Dad got a big promotion? Why couldn't we have stayed in Santa Monica, where the weather was sweet and the waves were sick?

But then I realized I could have a fresh start. I always used to be jealous when a new guy came to our school. He'd get all this attention. He was a mystery. He could be anybody. So maybe moving would be good. I'd be the stranger from a strange land. What girl could resist that?

Then I arrived.

First I was excited and nervous when the principal introduced me to Macallan, because she was pretty. Then she made it known within, like, 2.5 seconds that she had no interest in me whatsoever. You could've seriously given her a glass of milk and it would've been frozen in less than a minute. She was *that* cold.

So I figured we'd never talk again and I concentrated on the guys at school. Guys are always way more chill than girls anyway.

Right before lunch on my first day, I went up to this group of guys, introduced myself, tried to be calm, cool, and collected. But I'm pretty sure I stank of desperation. I was able to tell right away that Keith, this beast of a guy, was the alpha in our grade. He always had a group of three or four other guys around him, and they were all wearing some sort of Wisconsin team T-shirt. Keith had on a Badgers hoodie and jean shorts. He was close to five foot ten and he towered over everybody, including most of the teachers. He wasn't skinny and he wasn't fat; he was just big.

He studied me as I approached him, and said, "What's your deal?" before I had a chance to introduce myself. I made some small talk and felt like I was on a job interview.

Then I made a fatal error. I should've known better.

I admitted to being a Chicago Bears fan.

I'm pretty sure I heard actual hissing.

I figured whatever, they'd tease me, like guys do. That was what I was expecting, hoping. Because if guys teased you, you were kinda in.

But after I grabbed my lunch, not one person would look at me when I went to sit down. They were all too busy catching up with each other to notice the new guy standing there by himself. Instead of being this person everybody wanted to know more about, it was like I had leprosy or something. I kept being told that everybody in Wisconsin was so nice, but that wasn't the feeling I got. It was more like I was an intruder on their turf. I was only halfway through my first day and I was miserable.

Then Macallan came along.

She totally saved me from the public humiliation of having to eat alone on my first day of school. From then on, I ate with her and her friends.

At first I wasn't sure what to make of Macallan coming over on Wednesdays after school. The second we got to my house, she opened up whatever homework she had and would sit there and study until her dad came and got her. She only lightened up when I put on *Buggy and Floyd*. After a few Wednesdays, we started talking some more.

She was pretty cool. Like awesome cool, even though she could sometimes be cold.

One Wednesday, about a month in, she had to stay longer than usual. Mom came back from the store and said, "Macallan, sweetie, your dad just called me. He's running late, so you're going to join us for dinner. Hope you like stir-fry."

Macallan studied Mom from our place at the dining room table as Mom went into the kitchen and started unpacking her groceries. I tried to not laugh as Macallan's face scrunched up. She always did that when she was studying, be it math or my mom. It was pretty adorable.

"Hey." I tried to get Macallan's attention back to me. "Do you wanna play a video game or something?"

"I want to finish the outline for my English paper." She started scribbling in her notebook.

I picked up the tattered book she was reading. "*Miss Lulu Bett*?" I laughed. "You're writing your author report on someone who wrote a book called *Miss Lulu Bett*?"

Macallan reached her hand out for the book. "Can you please be careful with that? It's on loan from the library. It's rare."

I presented the book to her with both hands and a slight bow.

"And for your information, the author, Zona Gale, was born in Wisconsin and was the first woman ever awarded the Pulitzer Prize for Drama. It wouldn't kill you to learn a little bit about the history of where you now live."

"Uh-huh." That was usually my reply whenever Macallan tried to educate me on pretty much anything. I did okay in school, I got decent enough grades, but I wasn't the ultimate student like she was.

She kept her attention on her notebook. "Who are you going to write your report on? Dr. Seuss?"

"I *do* like green eggs and ham, Mac I am."

She grimaced. "I don't know why I even bother sometimes."

She pretended to get back to work, but I could see the corners of her mouth start to turn.

I cautiously picked up the book again. "Maybe I should read this. I wonder what kind of bet Miss Lulu placed."

Macallan groaned. "Mrs. Rodgers, do you need any help with supper?"

Mom popped her head into the doorway. "That's okay. I think I've got it covered."

But Macallan got up and went into the kitchen. "Are you sure?"

"Well, if you want, you can help me cut up some vegetables." Mom gave her a smile.

Great, does this mean I have to help? I thought. Leave it to Macallan to make me look even more like a slacker.

Mom pulled out some green and red peppers, zucchini, and mushrooms from the grocery bag and handed Macallan the cutting board and a knife. Macallan looked between the knife and vegetables like she was trying to solve a difficult equation. She held the knife to the pepper, first one way, then another.

At one point she looked up at me, probably hoping for help. Like I had any clue about cooking. I'd almost burned our house down microwaving popcorn the past year. It had smelled like charred popcorn for over a week. I'd been wisely banned from the kitchen ever since.

"Is there a certain way you want them cut?" she asked Mom.

Mom opened her mouth and then it was like I saw a lightbulb go on over her head. She went over to Macallan and showed her the different ways to cut everything. Macallan's green eyes were watching everything like she was gonna be graded on it.

"Thanks," she said quietly when they were through. "There isn't a lot of cooking at my house. Anymore."

It was then that I realized why Macallan was enamored with Mom. It was Emily who'd told me about the car accident — Macallan hadn't really said much about her mom to me. And I had no clue if I should've said something to her. Or asked. Like, what do you do in that circumstance?

Blimey if I knew.

Even though I was quickly becoming friends with Macallan and her group, I still felt like I needed some dudes in my life.

"What's up, California?" Keith came up to me after class in early November. "How's it hanging, bro?" But he said it like *brah*. I knew he was making fun of how I talked, but had he never heard himself? Everybody here had these nasally accents and overpronounced their vowels. I found it hilarious. "Saw you running 'round the track at gym. You're pretty fast."

"Thanks, man."

I debated bragging to him that I was faster when it wasn't so cold. Even though the snow from the first snowstorm of the year (which happened *before* Halloween) had melted, it was still freezing outside.

Part of me had already written off Keith and his group . . . and still I felt a little excited as Keith continued. "Yeah, maybe you could join our game sometime. Wide receiver or something. Do they even play football in La-La Land?" He laughed.

I decided to throw it right back at him. "I don't know, man. Ever heard of this little thing called the Rose Bowl? Probably not, since the Badgers haven't won it in years."

"Ouch." But Keith looked impressed.

I was a little rusty with the guy put-downs. Back in California, my buddies and I would spend hours ragging on each other, our families, the girls we liked. You name it. The bigger the put-down, the bigger the laugh. It was our own art form.

"Okay, California." Keith nodded to himself. "I guess I'll see you around. Don't let those chicks start braiding your hair or doing your nails. Real men play football."

"Yeah, totally." We did this awkward handshake thing that made me feel even more like a tool. But hey, at least he was talking to me. That was a start.

I could tell right away that Macallan was not in a good mood after school. Mom had a meeting that was running late, so we had to walk the twenty minutes to my house. She hardly talked to me during the walk and didn't even want to stop in Riverside Park. We always would stop in the park and goof around whenever we walked to my place. Even if it was cold out. But apparently not that day.

"Are you okay?" I finally asked her, mostly because the silence was super awkward.

She was all "Yeah, no . . . I don't feel well."

I saw her holding her stomach. I hoped she wasn't going to blow chunks in front of me.

Once we got home, she sat there. She didn't talk, she didn't want to watch TV, she didn't want anything to eat. She didn't even crack open a book to study. That's when I knew things were serious.

I started playing a couple video games; she silently watched from the couch. "Man, I tell you . . ." I looked at her and saw that she didn't look so great. I figured there was only one thing that could put a smile on her face. "Oi!" I called out in my best cockney accent. "You gonna just sit there or you gonna help me deliver . . . *a baby*?" Then I pretended to faint. It was classic Buggy.

She got up suddenly and went to the bathroom.

This was the problem with being friends with a girl. They could be so complicated. Like, was I supposed to guess what was wrong? Couldn't she give me a hint?

After I played a few more games, I realized she had been in the bathroom for an unusually long time. *Gross*. But what if she'd hit her head on the counter or something? I didn't want to bother her, but she *had* said she wasn't feeling well.

I approached the bathroom cautiously. "Ah, Macallan?"

"Go away!"

"Um, do you need —"

"I SAID GO AWAY!"

I was pretty sure she threw something at the door. Or she banged on the door. There was some noise that happened and it was clear she was not happy.

I didn't know what to do. My buddies back home never locked themselves in a bathroom.

Thankfully, Mom arrived home a few minutes later. At first she gave me a questioning look when she saw me staring at the bathroom door.

"Mom, I don't know what's going on. She's locked herself in there. I think she's crying. I swear I didn't do anything."

Mom's eyes got wide. "Go play video games."

Mom was always harping on me to stop playing video games. I went back into the living room before she could change her mind.

After what seemed like an eternity, Mom emerged from the bathroom.

"What's —"

She cut me off. "Listen, you're not to say anything to Macallan about this, or anybody at school. Do you understand me?" I wasn't used to her having such a harsh tone with me. "I need you to go to your room —"

"What?" I protested. "But I didn't do any —"

Mom snapped her fingers at me. *Great*. Now Mom was mad at me.

She lowered her voice. "I need to have a private conversation with Macallan's dad when he gets here. Now go to your room and I don't want to hear another word about this."

She folded her arms and I knew I had no choice but to do what she said.

I went up to my room totally confused. But I did know one thing.

I would never understand girls.

Oh, wow.

What?

I finally realized what happened that day.

You're *just* figuring this out now?

Yeah, I guess —

We're *not* having this conversation.

I can't believe I didn't realize you got —

What part of *we're not having this conversation* are you failing
to comprehend?

Do you think *I* want to talk about this?

Then why *are you* talking about this?

Uh, never mind.

We better hurry up and discuss something manly to get your
dude points back up.

Yeah. Uh, me like meat.

Chicks.

Football.

Fire.

Brats.

Pedicures.

Okay, you promised you'd never mention that. I had a blister, I was just . . .

Excuses, excuses.

You're the worst.

And you love me for it.

Yes, because I'm a total glutton for punishment. And one hundred percent pure man.

Stop laughing.

Seriously, stop laughing.

Macallan, it's not *that* funny.

CHAPTER THREE

"What if I got my hair cut?"

It was such a simple question Levi asked, but he had no idea what a what-if question did to me. It was a game I played with myself often. I had been doing it a lot that summer before eighth grade.

What if I hadn't been the one to show Levi around on his first day of school?

What if I hadn't seen his KEEP CALM AND BLIMEY ON button and opened up a conversation to see what else we had in common?

What if Uncle Adam had never mentioned Wednesday nights to Levi's mom?

What if his mom wasn't always around when I needed her?

But that's the thing with the what-if game — you really can never know the answer to the question. And maybe it's better that way.

Because underneath the surface what-ifs are much worse ones.

What if you hadn't forgotten your science book that day?

What if it hadn't been raining?

What if the other driver hadn't been texting?

What if Mom had paused for even three seconds before leaving that day?

What if?

"Ah, Macallan?" Levi waved his hand in front of my face. "What do you think?"

Levi removed the elastic from his hair and it fell a few inches down his back. "I feel like I need a new start for eighth grade."

I shrugged. "Might be nice."

"Even a few of my buddies back home have finally cut their hair."

Back home.

I noticed that even though Levi had been here for nearly a year, and his parents had no plans to move back to California, he kept referring to California as "back home." Like he hadn't fully been able to accept that this was now his home.

"So?" Levi asked.

It was then that I realized that he had walked us to the hair salon at the mall.

"Right now?"

He hesitated for a few beats. "Why not?"

Twenty minutes later, he was seated in a chair, his hair back in its familiar ponytail. The stylist grabbed it and then worked her scissors across. And in a few short seconds, the ponytail came loose.

Levi's hands went directly to the back of his head. "So

crazy." His voice sounded a little distant, like he couldn't believe it himself.

The stylist then handed me the hair. I studied it, thinking about how long he'd been growing it out. About how Levi had this whole other life before I met him. It hit me then about what it must've been like to really start over.

In some ways, I felt like I'd had to start over after the accident. But I still woke up in the same bed, went to the same school, had the same friends. There was something reassuring about waking up and knowing you were home. Hopefully, Levi would get to the point where he would feel like this was home to him.

I watched transfixed as more of Levi's hair came cascading down around his chair. The stylist didn't talk much, concentrating on the angles of his hair. When she was done cutting and styling, she turned Levi's chair around and he faced me. I hardly recognized him. His hair was now only about an inch long at the top and appeared darker, more dirty blond, probably since his "newer" hair hadn't seen much sun.

"What do you think?" Levi asked, eyes wide.

"I like it." I really did, even if it was the same haircut most of the guys in school had.

"Really?" He was staring at himself in the mirror. "You really like it?"

"Yes." I came over and couldn't help but run my fingers through it. "It's so short, but it looks nice on you."

Levi trembled at my touch, probably not used to having anything or anyone be so close to his neck.

He jumped out of the chair. "Let's go do something."

"Um, I thought we *were* doing something. We're at the mall."

He groaned. "You know that's not what I meant. Let's go play mini golf or go to the park or do something."

I glanced at my watch. "I can't. I have to get everything ready for tonight."

His shoulders sank down in defeat. "Okay. But Mom's really insisting on bringing something. And she only gets annoyed at *me* when I say you don't need anything."

"I don't want her to bring anything. This is my supper for you guys, a thank-you to your family for everything and a celebration for us that school's starting next week."

He shook his head. "You're the only person who gets excited that school's starting. Haven't we had an awesome summer?"

It *had* been a great summer. But I still craved the discipline the school year gave me.

I still needed the distractions.

I knew Dad was only trying to help, but I had everything planned down to the minute. I'd taken some cooking classes at the Y over the summer and had been getting better at it. I was making the salad while the lasagna was baking in the oven.

"You sure you don't need anything?" he asked for the seventh time.

"Seriously, Dad, I've got it. Please go do something, anything. Go watch TV with Adam."

He chuckled. "You sound exactly like your mother." It was the first time he'd mentioned Mom without getting sad. Instead, he was laughing. Of course, he was laughing *at* me, but I didn't have time to get upset about it. I had garlic bread to toast.

Luckily, the doorbell saved me, and Dad went to let Levi and his parents in. I heard a scattering of their greetings.

"Smells amazing!" Mrs. Rodgers greeted me in the kitchen. "I don't want to be in your way at all; I only wanted you to know that it all smells delicious."

Dad followed her with a bottle of wine in his hand, most likely a gift from Levi's parents. Then I saw Levi and almost didn't recognize him with his new haircut. It took me a second to realize he had flowers in his hand. His dad came behind him and gestured.

"Oh, yeah," Levi said, taking the cue. "Um, for the chef." He handed me the flowers, his cheeks ruddy from embarrassment.

"Thanks!" I hastily grabbed them.

Levi's dad winked at Mrs. Rodgers before giving me a hug. I was especially honored that Dr. Rodgers could make it. He worked such long hours, he usually didn't make it home in time for supper at his own house.

I shooed them all out of the kitchen so I could finish the meal. I couldn't help but smile when their voices and laughter drifted into the kitchen. It was nice to have joyful noise fill the house again. Every once in a while, I'd hear Adam groan and knew that Levi was trash-talking about the upcoming football season. You'd think he'd learn to keep his affinity for the Bears on the down low in Packers country.

The timer on the oven dinged just as I put the salad on the dining room table. We hadn't eaten there since my tenth birthday. There hadn't been much reason to celebrate or break out the good china in a while.

I looked over the table one last time before calling them in, making sure everything was in place. I felt my chest swell with pride as everybody came in and made a fuss.

Once everybody dug in, quiet fell over the table, except for the occasional compliment on the salad. I then served the lasagna with garlic bread before bringing out the chocolate cake I'd made for dessert.

"Cake, too!" Mrs. Rodgers patted her slim waist. "I'm glad I signed up for back-to-back spin class tomorrow morning!"

"Oh," I said, "the cake's only from a box. I haven't started taking any baking courses yet."

Her eyes got wide. "Honey, this is all amazing. I now feel like I need to up my game next time you come over for dinner."

I wanted to get up and hug her. Sitting around the table with everybody together made me realize how much I missed moments like that. I had forgotten what it was like to enjoy a meal together as a family. We'd gotten into the habit of making sandwiches or ordering in. We needed to have the TV on to fill in the silence. Because sometimes silence speaks much louder than words possibly could.

It was then that I knew this would be the first of many family meals we'd have together. I wanted to start a tradition with this new, growing family. Sure, the Rodgerses and I weren't related, but family doesn't have to be blood relations only. I think family is more a state of mind.

"You know, that reminds me." Dad put his finger in the air. "I've been meaning to have a conversation about the school year. I'm fine with Macallan being dropped off here on Wednesday, or any day really. She's been babysitting around the neighborhood and spending a lot of time here by herself during the summer, so she doesn't have to come over to your house."

Both Levi and I exchanged a look. I was pretty sure it was the same look, or at least I hoped it was. I liked going to his house and hanging out with him and his mom. I didn't like coming home to a house that was empty of people, yet full of memories.

Dad continued. "I think I've been a little overprotective. Our little girl is almost in high school. I can't believe it." Dad's eye drifted to a spot on the wall right behind me. I didn't need to turn around. I knew what was there: a photo of my parents' first dance on their wedding day. Dad had said something funny to my mom, because they were both laughing.

"But we love having Macallan over," Mrs. Rodgers said. I immediately felt better. "Right, Levi?"

I found myself holding my breath. I knew Levi wanted to make some more guy friends, but I hoped that wouldn't mean we couldn't still hang out. We talked about things that I couldn't with my girl friends. I liked not always obsessing over boys or what we were wearing the next day. Levi and I talked about real things. And he made me laugh more than anybody had been able to do in years.

Levi looked straight at my dad. "It wouldn't be the same without her, Mr. Dietz."

I was so relieved to hear his response that my eyes began

to burn. I got up and started clearing the table. Levi did the same. Once we set the plates down on the counter in the kitchen, he gave me that crooked smile of his.

"Dude, that was close. Blimey if I'd know what to do without you."

I felt the exact same way.

When we got our schedules for eighth grade, we discovered that the unthinkable had happened.

Emily, Levi, Danielle, and I had been split up for lunch. The only bright spot was that we'd been divided down the middle, so no one was left alone. Emily and Levi had first lunch, while Danielle and I were relegated to second lunch.

Emily was the most concerned about the lunch disaster, which surprised me. She'd always been the type of person who can walk into any room and start a conversation with a stranger. But she was uncharacteristically worried about eighth grade. All summer she kept saying that this would have to be our best year since none of us knew what would happen next year when we got to high school. A lot of this fear, I knew, was because Emily's older sister had gone, to quote Emily, from "it girl to *so* last season" once she got to South Lake High School.

I found myself extremely anxious on Levi's behalf while I was in history class. Was Emily sitting with him? Would she have abandoned him to sit with some of her cheerleading friends or Troy, her current crush?

My worries faded once I got to the hallway and saw Emily and Levi walking together, laughing about something.

"Hey!" Emily greeted me. "Stay away from the sandwiches at lunch — they're super soggy."

Emily winked at Levi. I felt a slight pang of jealousy rise up inside me. Which I instantly knew was silly. I wanted Levi and Emily to be friends.

Emily offered to walk me to my locker after we bid Levi good-bye. At least I'd see him later in English.

She linked her arm with mine. "You didn't tell me Levi got a haircut. He's so cute!"

"Oh" was the only response I could think of.

"So . . ." She let the word hang in the air. I knew what was coming.

I decided to cut her off at the pass. "What's going on with Troy?" I asked.

Emily had a new crush at the start of every school year. It always went like this: Emily declared a crush, she let her crush be known, the guy asked her out, they dated, and then she moved on to her next crush. She'd had eight legitimate boyfriends before the start of eighth grade. I always teased her that she'd run out of boys by the time we hit senior prom, but she promised she'd move on to college guys by then. I had no doubt this would be true.

"Ugh, Troy. I don't know." She gave me a look that made it clear she *did* know. "Levi's still this total mystery. Will you talk to him for me?"

I no longer had an appetite for lunch. Did I really want my best friend dating my — well, Levi had become one of my best friends, too. I had flashes in my head of having to be their go-between and their referee.

But then I realized that having my two best friends date could be a good thing. I sometimes felt I had to choose between hanging out with one or the other. Now we could all hang out in a group.

"Sure," I offered.

After all, what was the worst that could happen?

I don't think I give you enough credit for your positive attitude.

Yes, I'm Queen Optimist.

Well, I wouldn't put it that way.

I was being sarcastic.

Really?

I'd rather be cautious than assume that everything will just work out.

It's called being laid back.

Or unrealistic. But whatever works for you.

Exactly. Whatever works.

CHAPTER FOUR

Had I known that getting a haircut was going to make me a chick magnet, I would've shaved my head the second we arrived in Wisconsin.

I could tell that Emily was acting differently at lunch our first day back. But I assumed it was because Macallan wasn't around. Then she started doing all that stuff girls do to let you know they're interested in you. She threw her head back after I said something that wasn't *that* funny. Then she kept touching my arm and gazing into my eyes. At first, I thought that maybe she'd lost her mind over summer break. Then it dawned on me: Emily was flirting.

It wasn't that a girl had never flirted with me before. I'd had a few girlfriends back home. But ever since I'd arrived in Cheese Country, I hadn't had any girls pay any attention to me in *that* way.

I wasn't sure if I could tell Macallan about Emily. I mean, I knew Macallan and I were just friends, but people always talked about us like we were a couple. And when they did, Macallan usually scrunched her nose or did something that made it clear that the mere thought made her stomach turn. Which was a little harsh, but I knew where she was coming from.

Then when Macallan told me that Emily was interested in me and even helped me ask Emily on a date, it sorta cemented it. Macallan and I would never be like that. We were just friends. That's how she saw me. And maybe we were better off being only friends.

Which was cool. Especially since she was my best friend here.

I decided to surprise her with a special treat after school. I told Mom not to pick us up so it would be only the two of us.

"Where are we going?" she asked when I took a left turn instead of a right.

"It's a surprise." I grabbed her elbow and led her down the street.

"Okay." She sounded like she didn't trust me. "Have you decided what you guys are going to do on Friday?"

"Who wants to know?" I found myself asking that a lot that week. Anytime Macallan inquired about my upcoming date, I wasn't sure if she was curious or if she was getting intel for Emily.

"I am. I wanted to see if you needed any advice on what to do."

"Oh." I felt stupid for sounding paranoid. "I figured we'd get something to eat and see a movie. Is that too boring?"

"Sounds good to me. There aren't a lot of options around here."

"Yeah, same as back home."

Macallan's shoulders tensed. I was about to ask her if I'd done something wrong, but we were approaching our destination.

"Look!" I pointed up at the Culver's marquee.

Her eyes got wide. "Yes! You know Turtle's my favorite."

"Yes, I do. When we drove by this morning and I saw that it was the custard flavor of the day, I *knew* we had to come here. My treat."

Macallan smiled as we entered the restaurant and got in line. "Well, if it's your treat, I'm getting four scoops."

"As I expected. I think I may get a double ButterBurger, too. Gotta get more weight on." I patted my stomach. I wanted to be able to get onto a few teams next year in high school, but I was still the skinniest guy in our class. "I figured between you becoming a culinary master and all the deep-fried food in this town, I would've gained some weight by now."

"What a hardship." She shook her head. "Probably not the best idea to bring up in front of Emily the plight that is your inability to gain weight. She's tiny, but that doesn't mean she isn't self-conscious about her weight."

"That's so ridiculous. I've never gotten why girls have, like, the most messed-up idea of what they look like. Emily's body is, um . . ." This was the part where having your best friend be a girl got tricky. I couldn't really say "sick" like I would to my friends back home. "She's not fat. Nowhere near it. Neither are you. You're both, um, like, totally, ah . . . fine."

Macallan folded her arms over her chest. I decided it would be best to keep my mouth shut. I knew I made her uncomfortable. Macallan had recently started growing in, um, specific places. I couldn't help but notice that her shirts were fitting differently.

I was only a guy, and therefore human.

Very, very human.

I shook my head to try to get the image of Macallan in her purple V-neck shirt out of my head. Thankfully, it was our turn to order. Once we got our custards, we grabbed a table.

"So, any other topics of conversation I should avoid on Friday?" I asked while Macallan happily dived into her vanilla custard with caramel, chocolate, and pecans.

She nodded. "It's best to not talk about next year — she's really paranoid about going to high school."

As she explained about Emily's sister and everything, I made mental notes. There seemed to be a lot of things that I would have to be cautious about on Friday. It wasn't like with Macallan, where we could pretty much talk about anything.

Well, except current growth spurts.

"Yeah, I know, she —"

I stopped myself as Macallan's gaze settled on something over in the corner. I looked to see that some older kids were picking on an employee who was clearing off a few tables in the back room. They were pointing and laughing at him. I couldn't tell why until he turned around and I saw he must've had Down syndrome or something.

"Are those guys —"

She cut me off. "It's ridiculous. He shouldn't have to deal with this." Her cheeks became extremely flush.

"Should I go look for a manager?" I offered.

But Macallan had a different idea. She got up and headed over to the corner. I hesitated for a second but realized that I should be there in case she needed some help.

"Is there a problem?" she said to these three guys who were probably sixteen or seventeen.

"Oh, is that your girlfriend?" one of them asked.

I was used to the question being directed at me, but instead it was aimed at the guy who was trying to wipe down the table next to them.

"Oops." Another guy dumped his soda on the floor. "Better go clean that up, retard."

"EXCUSE ME?" Macallan's voice boomed through the seating area. Even some people in line started turning around to see what was going on.

"I wasn't talking to you." The guy started laughing.

Macallan stood in front of the table. "Well, you are now."

The guys were snickering and saying some things I couldn't make out. Then Macallan slammed her fists on their table. The guy who appeared to be the ringleader jumped a little.

"What's your problem?" Macallan asked, her entire body shaking. "All he's doing is working, minding his own business, cleaning up after slobs like you. He's making a contribution to society, which is a lot more than I can say about you. So who's the real waste of space in this scenario?"

A manager approached. "Is everything okay?"

The guys all mumbled that it was fine, but Macallan wasn't going to let them off that easily. "No, everything is not okay. These *gentlemen*" — she said the word with such disdain — "were harassing your employee, who is, I might add, doing excellent work."

"Yes," the manager, who looked to be around the same age as the guys causing the problem, said. "Hank is one of our best employees. Hank, why don't you take a break?"

Hank took his towel and trays from the table and walked away.

The manager waited for Hank to be out of earshot before he turned his attention back to the table. "I think I'm going to need to ask you gentlemen to leave."

They laughed. "Whatever. We were going anyway."

As they got up to leave, one of them brushed past me and said, "You need to learn to put a muzzle on your girlfriend."

I had been frozen the entire time. Macallan stood up to those three guys while I'd stood there like an idiot.

Macallan talked a little bit with the manager before he thanked her for stepping in. "It's great what you did. It's unfortunate, but it does happen."

"It shouldn't," Macallan said coldly.

Once we were back at our table, just the two of us again, I asked, "Are you okay?"

"No. I hate people like that. They think they're so much better than Hank. And they probably think they're better than you or me. What kills me is that those jerks get to walk down the street and nobody ever judges them. I can guarantee you that Adam works a lot harder in one day than those guys ever will in their lifetimes."

I'd never seen Macallan so mad. I knew she had very little tolerance for crap, but I'd had no idea how much it would set her off. "You're right," I told her. "And I'm really proud of you. I also know to never make you angry. That was something else."

A smile started to warm her face. "Sorry. I can't help myself."

"No, I'm serious. That was awesome. I never saw you as the confronting type. Lesson learned."

"Only when someone's being bullied, I guess."

"Let's get out of here. I think this calls for a *Buggy and Floyd* marathon."

"And some more custard."

That was the Macallan I knew. "Like I'd say no to you now."

She laughed as we headed back in line. I poked her in the ribs. "I'm telling you, no girl back home is as cool as you."

Macallan froze again. I immediately looked around to see if the guys were back.

"You know" — she turned toward me — "I understand that you spent your first twelve years in California, but *this* is your home now."

I wasn't sure why she was suddenly annoyed at me.

"I don't know —"

She interrupted. "You keep saying 'back home' all the time."

"I don't —"

She slouched her shoulders and did this low voice. " 'Yeah, my buddies *back home*, *back home* we did this, *back home* was all like this, and *back home* is awesome.' " I think she was doing an impersonation of me. But I so didn't talk with that exaggerated Valley accent she was doing. At least I hoped I didn't. She fixed her gaze on me. "*This* is your new home."

She moved forward and ordered her second custard. And I stood there thinking about what she had said.

Maybe I was still living in the past. Maybe I hadn't realized that this move was permanent. Maybe it was time for me to start living in the present, to embrace my new school and my new classmates. Maybe I hadn't made enough of an effort.

I had to face the fact that I was now a Wisconsinite.

I stopped looking at everything, especially school, as temporary. I was going to have to find a way to get comfortable at school and with the guys.

But first I had the little matter of my date with Emily.

We were sitting across from each other like we did every day at school for lunch. But this was different. Not just because we were at a pizza place before the movie. This was a date. And it wasn't *any* date, it was a date with the hottest girl in school *and* Macallan's best friend. This was a big deal.

Emily always looked pretty at school, but she went all out that night. I almost didn't know what to do when I met her at the mall. She had on this flowery dress and her hair had one of those sparkly barrettes in it. And every time she smiled at me, I got a little nauseous. Not the *I'm-gonna-hurl* nauseous, the *this-is-exciting* one.

I took an extra big sip of my soda as Emily smiled at me while we waited for our pizza. It was like she was expecting something witty, something more than our usual dissection of the school day.

"So . . ." She wrapped one of her loose strands of hair around her finger.

"So . . ." was my witty reply.

She reached her other hand out to me. "I'm so glad we're doing this."

"Me too."

Ugh. I swore I knew how to talk to girls. I talked to Macallan all the time. But I became worried that I'd used up all my small talk with Emily at school.

"I'm thinking of having a Halloween party," Emily said as her finger kept twisting her hair. I wasn't the only one who was a little nervous.

"That could be fun."

She nodded. "Yeah, especially since I was thinking that I'd invite all the guys, like Keith and Troy."

"Troy's cool." And the only guy who really gave me the time of day.

"Yeah, I feel like it would be good for you to spend some time with the guys."

I hated that it was so obvious to everybody how I wasn't "one of the guys" here.

I swallowed my ever-shrinking pride. "Thanks."

"Don't worry about it. Even I need to make sure to get in good with everybody."

That surprised me. Emily was one of the most popular girls in school.

She continued. "Especially Keith. Ever since we were little, he was always the one with the biggest circle of friends. He'd have the birthday parties everybody wanted to be invited to. That's not going to change for him. He'll have no problems fitting in next year. But the new school is going to be so big. I'm worried about getting lost." Her voice got quiet and she sank down in her seat a bit. Emily was usually so bright and bubbly, I felt like I was getting a deeper glance. "I don't know. I guess I'm thinking too much. I like the little circle we have now. And I feel things already changed so much with you moving here. I mean, I see Macallan less." Emily's eyes got wide, like she knew she shouldn't have said that.

Before I could say I didn't mean to take Macallan away from Emily, she jumped back in and said, "Not that I —" Then she fumbled for a second. "I like having you here. I hope you don't think it's that."

"No, I totally get it."

"But anyway . . ." She straightened up, and I knew the conversation was going to go back to the surface as well. "I know one person who won't have any trouble staying on Keith's radar next year." She raised her eyebrows playfully.

I had no clue who she was referring to. It certainly wasn't me.

"Macallan. He used to have the biggest crush on her. He probably still does."

I was pretty sure my eyeballs almost came out of their sockets.

Emily laughed. "Are you shocked that a guy would be interested in Macallan?"

"No, not at all." I actually found it strange that she never really talked about guys to me. I figured that was left to her girl friends.

"Yeah, it was sixth grade. But she didn't really have any interest in Keith or anything really after her mom . . ."

Emily's unfinished sentence hung over us like a dark cloud. I had always avoided the topic of Macallan's mom. I knew I was supposed to say how sorry I was if it ever came up. But it never came up. Macallan always talked to me about her dad, her uncle, and school — but she hardly ever talked about her mom.

"I don't know how she holds up as well as she does." I was surprised not only that these words came from my mouth, but how small my voice sounded.

Emily dropped her head a bit. "It was awful. It was so awful. I wish you could've seen Macallan when her mom was around. She was a different person. She was always smiling and laughing. It's not like she's all brooding now, but it was . . . a lot."

I was sure "a lot" was putting it mildly.

"But I have to tell you, she's gotten much better lately. Like whenever she starts talking about her cooking classes or the new recipes she's trying out. And also, I don't know if you realize how much your mom has helped her."

I nodded. It was pretty clear that Macallan adored my mom. It made me realize how lucky I was to have her around. To have both my parents around even though I got annoyed with how much time my dad spent at the hospital.

"Oh!" Emily started bouncing up and down in her seat. "I've got it! I think I should ask Macallan to make some food for the Halloween party. Wouldn't that be cool?"

"Yeah, she'll love that." I started thinking about all the food

Macallan's been making. "Do you think you can ask her to make those pulled pork sandwiches?"

"Definitely." Emily beamed.

We missed the seven o'clock movie and the one after that. Emily and I kept talking and talking. All the nerves we both felt started to melt away.

The only other time I got nervous that evening was when we said good-bye. Because I wanted to kiss her. Not just because she was cute but because, for the first time since I'd arrived, I had something to look forward to that didn't involve Macallan.

So I kissed her. And she kissed me back.

I wasn't going to let any other opportunities pass me by.

Generally when a guy gets a girlfriend, he usually ends up spending less time with his guy friends. But with Emily it was the opposite.

Before I knew it, I was starting to hang out with Keith and Troy. We went to the mall to get our costumes for Emily's Halloween party. We ended up grabbing a few slices and talking about sports. I hadn't had that much bro time since we left California. I even got excited when Keith picked on me for spending so much time with Macallan without making a move. I took it as a compliment that he was ribbing me. It meant I was in.

"Have I told you you're the greatest boyfriend?" Emily pecked me on the cheek as I put up the last of the fake cobwebs in her living room the night of the party.

"Not today." I winked at her.

She laughed before surveying the room for one last inspection before people arrived. We moved the furniture so there was a large area for people to hang out and maybe dance. We had a table set up on the side that had a punch bowl filled with "green slime" (which was basically green-colored punch), and chips, dip, pretzels, candy, and a lot of room left for Macallan's food.

Macallan, as with everything, outdid herself. There were mini "mummy" pizzas (where black olives were used as eyes), deviled eggs that had peppers sticking up like horns so the eggs looked like devils, cupcakes decorated with candy corn. And, of course, her famous-to-me pulled pork sandwiches.

"This all looks amazing, Macallan!" Emily hugged her.

Our group had decided to dress up with a *Grease* theme. The girls were going as the Pink Ladies while the guys were T-Birds. Emily was dressed as Sandy, with a leather jacket and all black with red shoes. Her normally sleek, black hair had been curled and teased beyond recognition. If Emily was Sandy, I guess that made me Danny. The guys had it easy; we only had to get white T-shirts and write *T-Birds* on them. Some of us had leather jackets — I'd borrowed my dad's old motorcycle jacket from when he had a motor-cycle; Mom had made him get rid of it once she got pregnant with me. The girls took pink T-shirts and wrote *Pink Ladies* in bubble let-ters and then wore poodle skirts with matching pink headbands and flip hairdos.

Mr. Dietz, Adam, and Emily's parents hung out in the kitchen while the party took over the living and dining rooms. Most of the guys who weren't in our group dressed up as football players or cowboys, which meant a plaid shirt and cowboy hat. It was the girls who'd gone above and beyond: beauty queen pageants, Catholic school-girls, or basically anything that required them to dress up and put on a lot of makeup.

Not like I was complaining.

"Hey, California!" Keith called out from his station in front of the TV. "You're up."

He threw me a gaming remote and I plunked down next to him.

We played video games for an hour or so. Every once in a while, he'd give me grief about my accent, my outfit (which was the exact same as his), my hair (which had been short for two months, but Keith had failed to notice), and pretty much anything I said. But I ate it up. This was how Keith treated his friends.

"Dude, next weekend. My house. You in?" Keith said after I finally beat him at a boxing game.

I had no idea what next weekend was or what we'd be doing at his house, but I agreed.

I had a girlfriend, an amazing best friend, and was finally becoming one of the guys.

Things were starting to look up.

Don't think I'm not offended that you were so desperate for some bro time.

Dude, you know I didn't mean it that way.

Dude. You make it seem like I forced you to have tea parties with my dolls and braid my hair.

You did start spending a lot of time in the kitchen.

That's funny. I don't remember hearing you complain while you were eating all the food I was making.

That's because you're the best cook in the state of Wisconsin. If not the entire culinary world.

Flattery will get you everywhere.

Don't I know it.

CHAPTER FIVE

Having your two best friends date wasn't as awkward as I'd thought it would be.

It was much, much worse.

The first month was a little uncomfortable. I had to watch what I said about one when I was with the other. Then one of them would pump me for information. Sometimes I had to be the go-between. I was even the third wheel on a lot of the first dates.

One time I went to get some popcorn before the start of a movie, only to discover them kissing (or, more accurately, sucking face) when I got back. I froze, not knowing what to do. For a split second, I debated turning around and ramming my head against the wall in hopes that I would get amnesia. Instead, I cleared my throat very loudly and they slowly peeled away. Thankfully, the lights dimmed down as I settled back in my seat, so I didn't have to make eye contact with either of them. I wasn't sure who should've been more embarrassed.

By the time November rolled around, Levi and Emily were inseparable. They were constantly holding hands and I swear I once saw them rubbing their noses together between classes.

I tried desperately to not be bitter. It wasn't that I wanted a boyfriend, but I couldn't help feel a slight sting when they didn't want me around. Instead of being a necessity, I was a hindrance. Anytime I asked one of them to do something, they already had plans with each other. And I wasn't included.

Sometimes I even wished they would break up. But then I figured that would make things even worse. What if I was forced to pick sides?

There was no way for me to get things back to normal.

So instead I spent more time with Danielle. "They're getting pretty serious, huh?" Danielle asked me as we waited in line to see a movie the week before winter break, just the two of us.

"Yeah." I was also getting tired of having to be the happy couple's spokesperson.

Danielle hesitated a second. "Don't you think . . ." She looked around to make sure we didn't know anybody. "Don't you think Emily's kind of slipped away a bit? I mean, I know she wants to spend time with her boyfriend. Duh. But she's never strayed this far from us. It's a bit much, you know?"

Yes, I did know. And times that by two for me. The only reason I still saw Levi on Wednesdays was that Emily had cheer practice.

"It *is* a little much." I only allowed myself to admit it to Danielle.

"Although, let's be honest, you'll probably have to remind me of this conversation when I finally get a boyfriend," she said dryly.

I tried to give her an understanding nod, although that just wasn't one of my priorities.

"Speak of the devils." I followed Danielle's gaze to the concession stand, where Levi had his arm draped around Emily. She leaned into his side and laughed at something he was saying.

I really liked Levi, I really did. But he was not as funny as Emily always pretended he was.

I groaned. "Do you think they're seeing the same movie as us?"

Dread came over me that I'd have to watch the *Emily and Levi Make-Out Hour* instead of the new Paul Grohl romantic comedy.

Danielle apparently read my mind. "Maybe we can sneak by them and sit toward the front?"

"Sounds good." We grabbed our tickets and headed toward the theater with our heads down. I felt my heartbeat pulsing quickly.

"Hey, guys!" I froze in my tracks upon hearing Emily's voice. For a split second, I debated pretending to not hear her, but Danielle was already heading over.

"Hey!" Danielle said cheerfully. "What are you guys doing here?"

I made a mental note to encourage Danielle to join the drama club.

Emily laughed. "Seeing a movie, silly!"

"Really? You didn't come here solely for the popcorn?" Danielle shot back.

"We're seeing *The Salem Reckoning*." Emily pretended to get chills down her spine. "Fortunately, I have this one to hold me tight." She beamed at Levi.

In the many years I'd known Emily, she'd always refused to watch a horror movie. Even the cheesy, so-bad-it's-funny kind. But I guessed she'd use whatever excuse she could get for PDL (public displays of Levi).

"Cool," Danielle said in a way that you could tell she found it the opposite of cool. "Well, I need to hit the little girls' room before I watch Paul Grohl be romantic and dashing for ninety minutes."

"I'll join you!" Emily grabbed Danielle by the arm and headed toward the restrooms.

"Hey!" Levi finally acknowledged my existence.

"Hey." I decided not to act like it wasn't awkward.

"Listen," he began. "I was thinking that maybe on Wednesday we could go grab a bite to eat and do some shopping. I totally need help picking out what to get my mom for Christmas."

I let the icicles that were beginning to form around me melt a little. He was making an effort. He was also asking me to help him with his mom's gift because I knew her better. I knew *him* better. Maybe I was being a little harsh. I wasn't being replaced. Because that was really what I thought was happening.

I was being foolish. Levi would never replace me.

We'd solidified our plans by the time Emily and Danielle came back from the restroom.

"Ready?" Emily grabbed Levi's hand.

"Yeah." Levi winked at me. "Have fun!"

"You too," I replied.

And I meant it.

Levi and Emily weren't the problem. My attitude was. Clearly, there was something wrong with me that I got threatened the second my two best friends didn't give me one hundred percent of their attention.

I knew right then what my New Year's resolution would be: to stop being so needy.

Once I gave myself an attitude adjustment, I began to smile whenever I saw Levi and Emily together. I remembered reading somewhere that if you smile at something, it automatically makes you happier.

So whenever Levi or Emily would bring up the other, I'd smile.

Soon it became an automatic response.

Levi and I were walking around the mall, our hands full of shopping bags. "So I was telling Emily" — *SMILE!* — "that I still haven't gotten used to this weather. I know everybody said last winter was particularly brutal, but I think this year's even worse. Like, negative degrees? How can it be so cold that the temperature doesn't even exist? Or, like, it's less than zero? How is that even possible? At least Emily has promised to keep me warm."

SMILE! I didn't know what else to do. I had to play a role, a happier version of myself so he wanted to still spend time with me.

Levi took my silence as an invitation to continue. "Yeah, so I was also kinda hoping you could help me pick out something for Emily."

SMILE!

"Oh, awesome!" Levi replied.

Even though I didn't say anything, my stupid grin made it seem like I'd be more than happy to help him pick out a gift.

Levi led me to a jewelry store. "You're so cool. I didn't know if it'd be weird to ask you. But who knows Emily better than you?"

He had a point. I didn't understand why I was freaking out over this. He was still the same Levi. It had only been a matter of time before one of us would start dating somebody. And in a way, this would stop people from thinking we were an item.

"Of course I'll help pick something," I conceded. "What were you thinking?"

"Well, I was here last week with my mom and saw this necklace and wanted to get your opinion." He led me over to a glass case full of different silver and gold necklaces. He pointed to one that was in the middle. "This one, but with an *E*."

My heart dropped when I saw which one he was referring to. It was a silver necklace with a small round pendant with the letter *P* engraved on it.

I took a few steps back. It felt like the floor was unsteady.

I heard Levi asking me if I was okay, but I couldn't concentrate. Everything around me was a blur. I couldn't hear what he was saying, I couldn't really do anything.

"I can't breathe, I need to . . ." I stumbled out of the store and quickly sat on the floor near a fountain. I put my head between my knees and tried to steady my breath.

"Macallan, what's wrong?" Levi's voice cracked. "Please, talk to me."

Sobs started to come out. I had trouble catching my breath. I needed to breathe. I needed to calm down and breathe.

But I couldn't. Just when I thought I was getting better, something always knocked me on my side. And it was always, *always* when I least expected it.

"Macallan?" He took out his phone. "Mr. Dietz, I'm with Macallan, I don't know what's going on. I think she's having some sort of panic attack."

Not my father, I thought. *Please don't bring my dad into this.*

I somehow found the strength to reach out and touch Levi's leg.

"Wait, she's getting my attention." Levi kneeled down. "Your dad wants to talk to you."

Levi lifted the receiver to my ear. "Calley, sweetie, what is it?" My father's voice was so worried. I hated that I was doing this to him. "Please talk to me."

"It . . . was . . ." I tried to calm myself down, but hearing Dad's voice made it worse. I took a deep breath. "Tell him about the necklace."

It was all I could get out, but enough for Dad to understand.

I watched Levi listen to what Dad was telling him. His face went white.

"I'm so sorry. I didn't know." His voice was so low and quiet. "I didn't know." I couldn't tell if he was apologizing to Dad or me. Probably both.

Of course he didn't know. How could he have? How could he have known that my mom had worn a very similar necklace with the letter *M* that my dad gave her the day they brought me home from the hospital? How could he have known that she wore it every single day? How could he have known that she died wearing it? That she was buried with it?

Levi hung up the phone and sat down next to me. He put his arm around me, and I leaned against his shoulder. "Your dad is on his way. I'm so sorry, Macallan. I'm so sorry that I didn't know. I'm so sorry that I had to remind you of something so hurtful. I'm so sorry I don't know how to help you with this big part of your life. If it's even possible. I'm so sorry that I don't know what to say right now."

He paused for a second, but just having him there, having him near me, was what I needed. "I know I've been a total idiot lately and haven't really been around. And I'm sorry for that, too. I know I don't know a lot, but what I do know is that I'm going to be here. Whatever you need, whenever you need it, you know you can count on me, don't you? Nothing will ever change that. Nothing. You do know that, right?"

I don't think I truly knew it for sure until that very instant. And even though my heart was being ripped apart by the memory of my mother, I let Levi's kind gesture help patch it.

I realized it was time for Levi to meet someone.

We were bundled up as we made our way up the hill. Levi had been quiet on the ride over. I wasn't sure how he would react, but I knew it was time for me to open up to him.

We approached our destination. Levi a few paces behind me, his head down.

"Levi, I'd like you to meet my mom." I stood next to her gray marble gravestone. "Mom, this is Levi. I told you about him." I brushed off some of the snow that was on top of the stone.

"Hi," Levi said softly.

"Come sit." I took out a blanket and laid it on the cold ground. "I wanted to bring you here so I could tell you a little about my mom." My voice started to quiver. This was what I'd been afraid of. It was really hard to talk about Mom without getting sad. But the therapist I saw after she died said it was important for me to talk about her. To share my memories of her with other people.

I wished Levi could've met my mom. She would've loved him.

"She . . ." I began, but felt the sting behind my eyes.

"It's okay," Levi said. "You don't have to if it's too hard."

"I want to."

"Can I start?" he asked. "Um, Mrs. Dietz, I'm Levi. I'm sure Macallan has told you all about me. And, well, none of it's true, unless she told you I'm awesome."

A small, grateful laugh escaped my throat.

"Yeah, I met her on the first day of school and you should know how nice she was to me. I've seen pictures of you at the house, so I know where she got her looks. And, um, she's a ridiculous student. It's kinda annoying really." He looked worriedly at me. "Is this okay?"

I liked that he was having a conversation with Mom as he would if she were here. "Yeah, it's great."

"Okay, so, like, when I first met her, I thought she hated me. You see, I had this long hair and I'm pretty sure she thought I was a hippie or something. But then she found out that I also liked this show, *Buggy and Floyd.*" He looked up from the ground. "Does she know what I'm talking about?"

I nodded. It made me happy that he used the present tense with Mom.

"Yeah, and from there we just kinda clicked. She's really the only person who's gone out of her way to make me feel at home. So thank you, Mrs. Dietz, for raising your daughter the way you did. She's awesome and I know that's because of you. I wish I could've met you, but I guess I have in a way. Because of Macallan. And just so you know, I'll do my best to protect her. And be there for her. Even if she does have the *worst* taste in football teams."

"Hey!" I swatted at him. "Mom's a *huge* Packers fan. He's only teasing, Mom."

He wrapped his gloved hand around mine. "It's okay that I joked?"

"Yes, she always jokes around."

"What else does she like?"

And that was all it took. For the next hour, I told Levi all about my mom. All I could remember. I laughed at so many of the memories. And not once did another tear fall. I still ached for her, but talking about her was keeping her alive inside of me.

I had no doubt that Mom was looking down at us and smiling.

Everything changed after that.

Maybe *change* wasn't the best word. But Levi and I were closer than ever.

Between my breakdown at the mall and the visit with Mom, Levi went above and beyond to make sure we spent time together.

It wasn't as if Levi put Emily aside for me. He knew he didn't have to make that kind of choice. He became more aware of how he was acting. The decisions he made. Whom he chose to spend time with.

Even though we constantly texted, he would call me at least once a day while he was in California during the holidays.

"I know how happy this is going to make you," Levi said during his call on New Year's Eve. "Everybody here is complaining about how much I'm talking about *back home.*"

"Do we think you have a case of the grass is always greener?" I asked.

He laughed. "Probably. But mostly the guys want to see more pictures of the coolest chick alive."

"You better be talking about me."

"Clearly. Even if said chick is having a rockin' party without me."

"Hey, I'm not the one who decided to spend the holidays two thousand miles away. And the party isn't going to be *rockin'* with everybody's parents there."

My dad had thought it would be fun to host a New Year's Eve party. So he invited some of his friends and their kids, and I got to invite my friends and their parents. At first I didn't think anybody would want to come to a party with their parents, but I guess it was the only way any of us would've been able to properly celebrate the ringing in of the New Year.

I had to hang up on Levi to get ready for our guests. Emily and Danielle came early to help me with the food. I made baked ziti, fettuccine Alfredo with chicken, spaghetti with turkey meatballs, garlic bread, and chopped salad.

Thankfully, the kids were relegated to the basement, so we got to have some privacy. I felt a little bad for Trisha and Ian, who were the kids of my dad's friends, since they didn't really know us. Trisha had moved from Minneapolis, and Ian was a year older than us. When I'd heard he was coming, I immediately thought he'd be upset being stuck with young kids, but he came downstairs with a smile on his face and introduced himself to everybody. Trisha stayed in the corner watching TV with Emily's younger sister and Danielle's brother for the first hour or so.

"I wish Levi was here." Emily sulked. "Now who am I going to kiss at midnight?"

"Don't look at me," Danielle teased. "I'm going to try to work my magic on that freshman. He's a hottie. Off to show him my winning personality." Danielle went over and sat down next to Ian.

"You don't think Levi's going to be with a girl tonight?" Emily asked me.

"No, he's hanging with his bros," I reassured her. I'd had to do that every day since Levi had left. I knew he could be trusted. He wasn't the cheating kind.

"What's up, guys?" Troy came over with a plate full of chips. "Are we going to break open any of these games or what?"

Emily smiled at him. "Good idea! Games!"

She guided Troy over to the table where we had some old-school board games set out.

Emily's sister grabbed checkers and brought them over to Danielle's brother on the other side of the room, where they set up shop.

"Oh, they're too cool to hang out with their older siblings." Emily laughed. "I remember being in fifth grade and thinking I was *da bomb*."

Troy looked up from the game of Monopoly he was examining. "I don't know — I think you're *da bomb* now."

Emily threw her head back and let out that exaggerated giggle she did around guys.

Troy scratched his head, leaving his wavy brown hair sticking up in places. His smile was so big, I noticed for the first time that he had a dimple in his right cheek.

But for some reason, I had a feeling it wasn't the first time Emily had noticed this. After all, he'd been her crush before Levi.

"Oh, you." Emily swatted at his hand. Then she nervously twisted up her long hair and let it fall back in place. She finally brought her attention back to me. "Do you want to see if anybody else wants to join us or . . ."

At first, I thought she was trying to get rid of me. But then I realized I was being paranoid. Emily was inviting others to join them, which was something I should've been doing. In an effort to be a good hostess, I went over to the sectional where Danielle, Ian, and Trisha were sitting. "Do you guys want to play a game or watch a movie? We still have two hours until midnight. Or I can get you some more food from upstairs."

"A movie would be cool," Trisha answered.

"Okay. You guys can pick it out."

Danielle joined Trisha while she went through the movie selection.

Ian got up. "I think I'll grab us some more food."

I went upstairs with him. We heard the parents' laughter filling the living room. It seemed like they were having a more rockin' time than we were.

"I can't believe you made all this food," Ian said when we got to the kitchen. He took another big helping of the ziti. "It's so good."

"Thanks." I put some more garlic bread in the oven. "I really like doing it."

"I can tell you this much — you aren't going to like the food in the cafeteria next year."

I debated asking him more about high school, but I didn't want to seem so . . . young. "I guess I'll start packing my lunches, then" was the only way I could think to respond.

He took a big forkful of pasta. His dark hair fell in front of his eyes briefly before he whipped his head to the side.

"Yeah, and if you need any advice on what classes to take next year or teachers to avoid, just ask." He smiled broadly at me, a speck of tomato sauce staining his upper lip.

"Thanks." I realized I wasn't adding much to the conversation. I'd apparently forgotten how to talk to guys who weren't Levi. It wasn't that I never talked to guys; it was that I never felt compelled to make small talk solely for the sake of small talk.

Ian helped me cut up the bread and we brought some out to the adults, who were all busy having a debate over politics. When we got back down to the basement, we found Danielle and Trisha watching *Sixteen Candles*.

"I've never seen this movie before," Ian said as he plunked down on the couch next to me.

"It's a classic," Trisha told him. "My mom was apparently obsessed with it when she was my age."

I looked around the room. "Where did Emily and Troy go?"

Danielle took a piece of garlic bread from Ian's plate. "You didn't see them? They went upstairs to get something."

"Oh." We must've missed them when we were in the kitchen.

The four of us sat back and watched *Sixteen Candles* with occasional commentary on the fashion and the hair.

"You should see this photo of my mom." Danielle laughed. "She had, like, these tight ringlets in her hair and, like, her bangs stuck up about a foot. She swears it was cool back then, but I don't know what planet that would be considered anything but a hot mess."

"At least some decent music came from that time," Ian offered.

"Yeah," I agreed as I shut off the movie. I glanced at the clock. "We have fifteen minutes 'til the New Year!"

We turned on the TV to watch the ball drop at Times Square. It was only two years ago that I'd realized they delayed the feed from New York City an hour for the central time zone. Before then I'd thought they redid the ball drop for every time zone. I'd thought that was the coolest, to get to celebrate the New Year four times.

"Okay, seriously. Where are Emily and Troy?" Danielle asked.

I'd almost forgotten about them. "They probably got caught up in the grown-up talk. I'll go save them."

I went upstairs and didn't see them in the kitchen or the living room. I checked the powder room and they weren't there. I went upstairs and saw that my bedroom door was closed.

Never did it dawn on me that I should've knocked. Why would I have knocked on my own door?

"Hey, Em, are you guys —" I froze at what I saw.

Emily and Troy were kissing on my bed.

They both bolted upright. "Oh, hey, we were, um . . ." Emily bit her lip, probably trying to think of a lie that I'd believe. And I desperately wanted to hear something that would make me think I hadn't just witnessed my best friend cheating on my other best friend.

Troy said the smartest thing he could at a time like this. "I'm going to head downstairs."

Emily and I were silent after he left. Only the sound of laughter from the oblivious adults could be heard.

Emily finally spoke. "I know."

"You *know*?"

"I was stupid, it's just . . . it's New Year's Eve. I'm at a party. Is it so wrong that I wanted to have some fun?" She sank back onto my bed and put her head in her hands. "You can't tell Levi."

I couldn't think of a response. I was so shocked at how quickly the evening had changed.

She finally looked at me. "Can you please say something? Anything?"

I was afraid to open my mouth because I had no idea what would come out. Eventually, I couldn't take it anymore. "How could you?"

Emily shook her head. "I don't know. I mean, you know I used to like Troy. And we were flirting while we were playing, and I think he's cute. You *know* I used to like him."

"*You* have a boyfriend. And need I remind you that he's my best friend."

"I thought *I* was your best friend."

"You both are." But in that instant I certainly felt closer to Levi.

"Levi's great. But he's not here." Emily sank back on my bed, her feet dangling toward the floor. It was a position we'd both been in often. A physical position. This awkward emotional position I was currently in was a first. And not one I cared to repeat.

"So that makes it okay?" I asked.

"No, it doesn't." I was relieved that this was her answer. "I'm confused, that's all."

"About what?"

"Everything." She started to tear up. "I'm getting freaked out over next year. I don't think you realize how much things will change. Everything's going to change. It already has."

I sat down next to her so we were both staring up at the glow-in-the-dark stars on my ceiling. "Emily, you've got to let this go. You're not your sister."

"You know what happened with her. You saw. Cassie had all these friends when she was our age. Then she went to that big school and got lost. She'd come straight home freshman year and go into her bedroom to cry."

"But your sister's a lot quieter than you. You're more outgoing. You'd never be lost. And you have me." I wanted to add that trying to date the entire male population at our school at the same time wasn't going to make things better for her, but I knew this wasn't the time. What she needed was reassurance. "Not everything is going to change."

"Our group will be broken up. I used to be your only best friend, and don't think it hasn't hurt me that you've been spending more time with Levi."

I couldn't believe she was trying to turn this on me. Yes, I spent a lot of time with Levi. But *she* was the one who canceled plans with me to spend more time with him.

"And I get worried for you, Macallan. I do. Levi's great. But when he gets to high school, do you think he's going to be fine hanging out with only you? He's going to have all these friends, and I don't want you to be left alone."

"I didn't think I was going to be left alone." My throat tightened. "I thought you were my best friend, too." I turned my head in time to see her cringe.

"I *am* your best friend. But sometimes I question where your loyalty lies."

I stayed motionless on my bed, repeating Emily's words in my head. This was an impossible situation — was she really asking me to make an even more impossible choice? A knot began forming in my stomach. Could I really choose between the two? I'd known Emily for as long as I could remember. She was always happy to lend a hand when I needed girly advice. She had been there for me during the absolute worst time in my life.

Maybe Emily was right. Maybe I had been neglecting her since Levi had come to town. But did that make what she was asking me okay? Levi and his family had meant the world to me the past eighteen months. I couldn't imagine my life without him. But I felt the same about Emily.

Why was this landing all on me? This was exactly the situation I'd been worried about when they'd started dating. What would happen after they broke up?

I tried to keep my voice steady. "Are you giving me an ultimatum? That I need to be loyal to you?"

"I don't know what I'm saying." Emily sat up. "I'm obviously really confused. I'm so sorry. I feel horrible. I don't want to come between you and Levi, and I don't want Levi to come between us."

Yeah, I thought, *you're one kissing session too late on that one.*

Just then, I heard everybody downstairs counting down. While they happily rang in the New Year, I was trying to figure out how to salvage the two most important relationships in my life.

A "HAPPY NEW YEAR!" chorus erupted below.

"Hey!" Emily hugged me as I got up. "Happy New Year, Macallan! Can we make a fresh start? I promise to figure out what to say to Levi. I don't want you to worry about it. It's my problem, not yours."

All I could do was hope she was right.

Emily got up off the bed and clapped her hands. "Come on, Macallan! It's the New Year, a new start, a new beginning! Anything's possible."

I felt a sense of dread envelop me. Because anything *was* possible. But those last ten minutes had made me realize that maybe that wasn't a good thing.

New beginnings are overrated.

I know. I'll never understand why everybody puts so much emphasis on January first. There are three hundred and sixty-four other days in the year that you can make a change.

Or make a fresh start.

Or start a diet.

You're not allowed to starting cooking with low-fat ingredients.

Obviously.

Or, you know, hide something from me ever again.

Well, you're never allowed to leave the state of Wisconsin again.

Yep. That totally seems fair.

I can only control so much.

If only you could be in charge of the world.

Finally someone gets it! I *should* be in charge of the world. Wouldn't life be so much better?

Obviously. First law as Queen of the World?

Banishment of the Chicago Bears.

On second thought.

Hey, it's my world. I get to rule it as I see fit. What if I made it so you'd be the standard against which all guys are judged?

Like you don't already do that.

Right. Question: How many suns are there in your world?

CHAPTER SIX

I practically ran off the plane the second we touched down in Milwaukee.

It was funny. I had spent the last eighteen months wishing to be in California, but once I got there, I realized all I'd left behind in Wisconsin. Sure it was cool to get to hang with my old buddies. But I missed my girls: Macallan and Emily. I guess most guys would've thought I was a player since I had two girls. But they meant completely opposite things to me.

Macallan was kinda my better half. The yin to my yang. Um, that sounded way dirtier than I meant it to.

And Emily was an awesome girlfriend. She radiated this positive energy. I could tell she was always happy to be around me. What guy wouldn't want that?

Although I have a confession to make. I lied to Emily over the break. I told her I wasn't getting back until Saturday evening, when in fact my flight arrived in the afternoon. I only did it because I wanted to see Macallan first. I knew Emily would want to see me right away, but I still owed Macallan her present.

I had a stupid grin on my face when I rang the doorbell at the Dietzes' house.

"Hey!" I picked up Macallan in a tight grip when I saw her.

"Hey back!" She laughed as I put her down. "How was the culture shock?"

I walked into the foyer and started taking off my many layers. "It was more the shock of getting off the plane just now and being hit with the cold air. I was wearing flip-flops on New Year's Eve."

Macallan winced slightly.

"Everything okay?"

She shook her head a little too vigorously. "Um, yeah. Ah, it's only that, um, it's strange to think of celebrating the holidays in the heat. Mom used to get so mad if there wasn't snow on the ground at Christmas."

Macallan's odd behavior was now making sense. I knew how much her mom loved the holidays, so this time of year must've been particularly hard on her. Which probably also explained the mess in the kitchen. There were pots and pans everywhere. Macallan cooked a lot when she was trying to clear her mind. Or trying to distract herself from something. And with us being on winter break, she didn't have homework to fill that void.

I rubbed her arm, thinking it would be the best way to comfort her. Ever since we'd gone to the cemetery, I knew it was okay for me to bring up her mom. I was so honored when she took me. It cemented how important our relationship was. But I also knew that if she wanted to talk about it with me, she would. It was getting to the point that I could read Macallan pretty well. I knew when she needed to be prodded into saying something and when she needed to be left alone. And the look on her face screamed, *Leave it alone.*

"Well, I'm used to the good weather year-round," I reminded her. "And I'm sorry I asked you to lie to Emily about when I was coming back."

"Yeah . . ." She started cleaning up the counter. "Do you want something to eat?"

I'd never passed an opportunity to eat anything she made. Macallan put together a plate of fudge brownies, Rice Krispies treats, and a slice of pecan pie.

I reached into my bag and pulled out her present. "Merry Christmas, a week late."

She hesitated before she opened it. "It's not a Bears hat, is it?"

I laughed. She'd given me a Green Bay Packers knit hat to help me "fit in." Everybody had gotten a big kick out of that, especially Adam. But after all the ribbing, she'd also given me a coupon for a homemade meal of my choice. It was my favorite gift that year.

She started unwrapping the box. She began laughing the second she saw one of the pictures on the DVD case. "I can't believe you got me —" She stopped herself as she saw the inscription on the front. "How did you . . . ?" Her mouth was practically on the floor. This made me extremely happy.

"My buddy's dad knew the producer on the show. I called in a favor."

She stared down and then read the inscription on the *Buggy and Floyd* DVD from the actor who played Buggy: *Blimey if I don't fancy me a glass of Macallan.*

"I couldn't figure out if it was genius or dirty," I confessed.

"Genius!" Macallan started laughing. I loved it when she laughed. She had two kinds of laughter: One was a normal chuckle, while the other was this boisterous, head-flailing-back laughter. If I had only one goal in life, it would be to make her laugh loudly every day. And that day, my mission had been accomplished.

"This is the greatest, thank you!" She flung her arms around me. "You can have as many meals as you want, whenever!"

"I'd like that in writing, please."

Her head fell back again as she laughed and, I kid you not, my heart actually soared.

"So." I started playing with her hair, which changed color depending on the season, like a tree. It was currently dark brown with a red overtone. "Tell me everything. How was New Year's?"

The smile quickly vanished from her face. I should've known better to keep bringing up something that reminded her of her mom. "It was good," she said. "Um, when are you seeing Emily?"

I checked the clock. "I told her my flight got in right about now, so I should call her soon."

"Yeah, you should call her. I know she really wants to see you."

This was why Macallan was the greatest friend in the world. I hadn't seen her in ten days, yet she wanted to be sure I saw my girlfriend.

"Do you want to come with me to see her?" I wasn't ready to say good-bye to Macallan just yet.

She shook her head. "No, you guys should have some alone time."

"Come here." I gave her a huge hug. "You're the best. You know that, right?"

She gave me a meek smile. I didn't want to leave, because there was clearly something wrong. But maybe what she needed was some time alone. She was trying to get me out of the room fast enough.

"So are you." Her eyes were so sad.

While I walked the seven blocks to Emily's house, I couldn't get Macallan out of my mind.

My best friend needed me and I was going to figure out what to do to help her.

But first I had to see my awesome girlfriend.

"LEVI!" Emily screamed before I even had a chance to get to the door.

She ran out in the cold and kissed me, which helped warm me considerably.

"You didn't call me when you landed; I was getting worried!" She held my hand and led me inside.

I'd been so preoccupied with Macallan that I'd forgotten to even warn Emily that I was coming. "I had to drop something off at Macallan's first," I said. I didn't want to lie to Emily anymore.

"Oh, you saw Macallan?" She smiled widely. "What did you guys talk about?"

I shrugged. "Just the usual. Plus, I still needed to give her the Christmas present."

"Oh, right, that DVD thing?" She led me to the couch and asked me all about my time in California. She hardly let me ask her anything about what she'd done over break. It wasn't like we hadn't texted while I'd been away, but she kept wanting to know every detail about my trip.

"Hey, how was the New Year's Eve party at Macallan's?" I finally managed to ask.

"Why?" she fired back quickly.

"Ah, only curious. Macallan didn't say much."

"Oh." Emily looked relieved. "It was great, a really good time." She bit her lip. "Um, there's something I should probably tell you. It's totally not a big deal. You know Troy was there and whatever. I was giving him the tour of the house and we were in Macallan's room. I guess the door was closed . . ."

I felt a tightness start to form in my chest.

"Anyway, we were talking and it was getting late and we were lying on the bed talking and Macallan walked in. It obviously startled us, but Macallan thought we were doing something, but it was all innocent. I swear. I just missed you so much."

I didn't know what to say. Mostly because I couldn't believe Macallan hadn't tipped me off. Even if it *was* nothing.

"But it's a new year, a new start." Emily leaned in and was only inches away from me. "I shouldn't have talked to Troy or given him a tour, but, like, I don't know. I wasn't even going to tell you, but I didn't want to keep anything from you." She started rubbing my leg. "Forgive me?"

She started to kiss me. At first I hesitated. Not because Emily was a bad kisser, but there was so much information to process. But I gave in. If it were a big deal, Macallan would've said something. There was no way she would've seen Emily cheating and not tell me.

I *thought* I could trust Emily, but I *knew* for certain I could trust Macallan.

Ahem.

You know you don't need to say a single thing to make me feel bad about that.

I know.

But you're going to anyway, right?

Nope.

No?

Oh, Macallan, one of us has to be the bigger person about such things.

You've got to be kidding. Since when are you the bigger person about *anything*?

Since I forgave you for your betrayal.

You're right.

Wow! Did that actually work? I'm right? About something? It's a Christmas miracle!

You're pretty proud of yourself, aren't you?

Well, it is nice to be right about something for once.

Don't get used to it.

Oh, I won't. You know I won't.

CHAPTER SEVEN

It was torture. Complete and utter torture.

I don't think I breathed the night Levi left my house to go talk to Emily. I stared at my phone, convinced I was going to get a phone call from a newly heartbroken version of him.

The phone did ring, but it was Emily.

"Please," she begged. "I know I made a mistake and the only person the truth would hurt is Levi. You don't want to hurt him, do you?"

No, I didn't. But *I* wasn't the one who'd cheated on him.

"I promise you that I'll never do anything like that again, and if I do, you'll never have to speak to me for the rest of your life. I wouldn't expect you to, either." I could practically hear her pulse over the phone. "I really like Levi and I don't want him to break up with me. Please, Macallan."

I didn't like having secrets. Secrets only ended up hurting people.

She continued to plead. "You're my best friend. If I can't trust my best friend, who can I trust?"

I bet Levi thought the same thing.

"I've known you for forever, we've been through so much. Can't you please forgive me so I can forgive myself?"

That hit a nerve. I never thought about what Emily was going through, how hard this was for her. Although it *was* her fault.

"Please, Macallan, I'm begging. If I was there right now, I'd be on my hands and knees. If that's what you want, I'll be there in two minutes to grovel in person."

I was so torn. Could I take her word that it would never happen again? I knew the truth would likely crush Levi. Maybe, I figured, it would be best to pretend it had never happened.

"Okay," I said quietly.

There was a pause on the other end. "Really? Oh my goodness, Macallan. Thankyouthankyouthankyou! I'll make this up to both of you, really."

"Please treat Levi well. He deserves it."

"I will! I promise! I love you!"

I should've felt relief when I hung up the phone, but all I felt was dread. As much as I wished to erase that night from my mind, I knew that some memories were harder to forget than others.

Especially the painful ones.

I'd told myself many lies over the years. The most frequent was "you'll be fine."

Yes, everything was going to be fine.

You're going to grow up without a mother, but you'll be fine.

You'll wake up every morning and realize it wasn't a nightmare, it was real. But you'll be fine.

You'll have to carry around a secret that could destroy your two closest friendships, but you'll be fine.

And I thought I was a horrible liar.

One thing I had become very good at was avoidance. Avoiding Emily and Levi together. Avoiding talking about their relationship with either of them. Avoiding any topics involving parties, Troy, my bedroom, emotional scars, etc.

I managed to do it for over three months. Three months of not being able to be completely honest and open. Three months of having to watch every word I said, every move I made. Three months of pure, unadulterated torture.

As the snow melted and hints of sun started poking through the clouds, I thought maybe I would be able to put it completely behind me by the time summer arrived. I even saw a flower start to bloom while I was on my way to lunch in early April. I figured that had to be a positive omen.

Danielle waved to me from our regular lunch table. "Guess who I ran into last night."

"Who?" I pulled out my carrots and homemade hummus.

"Ian." She wiggled her eyebrows.

"Ian?"

She sighed. "Ian Branigan, from your New Year's Eve party?"

Oh. I'd almost forgotten there were other things that had happened that night.

"Yeah. He seemed *very* interested in what you were up to these days."

"So?"

"She says 'so?'" Danielle said to nobody in particular.

"Oh, I'm sorry. He asked about me? Should I get the wedding registry ready?"

"She mocks."

"Yes, *she* does."

Danielle reached across and helped herself to some of my hummus. "I simply thought you'd be interested to know that a very cute boy was interested in you. And I may have mentioned that we were going to go to his track meet this Friday."

"We're going because Levi wants to check it out."

"Yes, and while Levi checks out the team he wants to be on next year, *you* can check out Ian."

"He's a freshman."

Danielle tapped her index finger against her lips for a moment. "Good point. What would someone at the bottom of the high school food chain want to do with a gorgeous girl like you?"

"That's not what I meant." I didn't know what I'd meant exactly.

"All I'm saying is that he asked about you and that I said we'd be at the meet on Friday. No big deal."

"Right." I *was* making too big a deal out of it.

"Yes, no big deal at all." Danielle gave that smirk that let me know another one of her patented zingers was coming my way. "Now do you care to explain why your cheeks are so red?"

I always went to Levi's mom when I had a question of the female variety. But I didn't feel comfortable asking her what to wear to the track meet. I knew she would've probably been excited to help me, but I wasn't sure how excited she would be about my having feelings for somebody. Anytime Levi and I got into one of our little bantering conversations, I'd catch our parents giving one another those looks. Those *aren't-they-so-cute* looks. I was sure she'd be happy, but another part of me thought she wanted Levi and me to be together.

As much as I didn't think Ian was into me that way, I also realized that maybe I wouldn't be so preoccupied with Emily and Levi's relationship if I had one of my own. I did love distractions.

So I went to the only other person I trusted for girly advice: Emily.

I sent her a quick text that I was coming over, and left for her house. I was too excited to wait around for a response. It wasn't unusual for either Emily or me to stop by the other's house unannounced.

I was only a few steps away from the front door when it opened. For a split second I assumed Emily had seen me approaching the house. But someone else stepped out of it.

Troy.

"Hey, Macallan!" he greeted me. "How's it going?"

The door swung open and Emily jumped outside. "Hey, what a surprise!"

"I sent you a text," I stammered, trying to make sense of what I was witnessing.

Emily waved her hand dismissively. "Oh, no worries. Troy was getting the, ah, homework assignment we had in history."

Troy looked at her weird. "Yeah, sure. Catch you later." He walked down the street like he didn't have a care in the world.

"It's not what it looks like," Emily assured me once we got to her room.

"Then what was it?" I asked. I refused to sit down next to her on her bed. I folded my arms and waited for her explanation.

"Troy and I were just hanging out. Honestly. I'm trying to get to know him better. Last time I checked, that wasn't a crime."

"What about Levi?"

"Levi knows." She picked up a magazine on her nightstand and started flipping through it like we were done with this conversation.

We were not.

"Levi knows what?" I prodded.

"He knows that Troy was coming over today to study. They're friends."

"Yeah, some friend."

"It's complicated."

I was so sick of that excuse. Because that's all it was: an excuse. "Then explain to me. Because honestly, Emily, I have no idea what's going on with you lately."

Emily dropped the magazine as if I was being the unreasonable one. "I'm just confused, that's all. And I'd appreciate it if you weren't so hard on me. We can't all be perfect like you."

I glared at Emily. I didn't appreciate that she was trying to turn this around on me. This had nothing to do with me. Although it felt as though it did.

She could tell that I was still waiting for a response. "Listen, I like Levi, I do. He's so sweet and cute. But I also like Troy. So I'm spending time with Troy just to see if, you know . . ."

"No, I don't know." I could practically hear the icicles cover each syllable as they came out of my mouth.

Emily sulked. "I like them both. I want to make an informed decision before I choose."

"Are you being serious right now? What you're doing to Levi is completely unfair."

"I know." Emily looked sad. "I do. I promised myself that I had to make a decision by graduation."

"That's over a month away," I reminded her.

"Please, you're not going to tell Levi what's going on, are you?"

I got up and headed for the door. "Really, Emily? I wouldn't even know where to start."

Where to start?

I got it. When somebody tells you you're seeing things that would get them in trouble, you're most likely not imagining it.

How about when someone tells you she's hanging out with someone she used to have a crush on just to study, don't believe her.

So true.

Or if your best friend says she's going to a track meet solely to keep you company, you don't assume she's there to hit on another guy.

That was *not* why I went.

Who's lying now?

I'm *not* lying. I can't help it that my pale skin and sparkling charisma make me irresistible to men. What was I supposed to do, be rude?

Whatever.

CHAPTER EIGHT

I thought having a girl best friend and a girlfriend would've given me some understanding of how the female mind worked.

Yeah, not so much.

Things became really bizarre between me and Emily. She began being extra enthusiastic around me. And any time I mentioned Macallan's name, she would laugh and then change the subject.

Macallan wasn't much better. It used to be that whenever I mentioned Emily's name, she'd smile. Now she winced.

A buddy of mine in Cali gave me his theory that they were both in love with me and fighting over me.

Yeah, right. Maybe if this was a dream.

I avoided talking about Macallan with Emily and vice versa. As long as Emily didn't come up, things were normal between Macallan and me. So I was looking forward to going to the high school's track and field meet with Macallan and Danielle.

We sat in the bleachers with Macallan in the middle. She held up her hand to shield the sun from her eyes. "Glad I brought sunblock," she said before riffling through her bag and applying lotion to her face and arms. Macallan's hair in the spring and summer was my favorite; in the sun it was almost bright red with an orange under-tone. But if we went inside it looked like it did in the fall.

She continued to squint. "Here, take my sunglasses," I said. I had a hat on so at least the sun wouldn't bother me as much.

"Oh!" Danielle elbowed Macallan. "Look — Ian's stretching."

I couldn't see Macallan's reaction, but whatever it was made Danielle laugh.

Who's Ian? I thought. I looked over and saw some guy stretching his hamstrings and doing a quick jog with his knees up. Did Macallan know him? I didn't remember her ever talking about an Ian.

I studied Ian. He was tall and skinny with dark hair that curled up at the ends. I guess he'd be considered handsome, if you liked lanky guys. I mean, I could be considered lanky. So would I be Macallan's type?

He took to the starting line and was in the middle lane with seven other guys.

"What times are we looking for?" Macallan asked me. She didn't seem too interested in him. Maybe Danielle was the one with the crush?

"I usually do the four-hundred in fifty-five seconds. So, hopefully, they're around that time."

The shot fired off and the runners began sprinting. I noticed that they held their chests out more than I do. I have a tendency to slouch when I run. Not good for speed.

Ian was in a close second, and as they rounded the final corner of the track, he sped up.

"GO, IAN!" Danielle stood up and cheered. She grabbed Macallan to join her.

"Could you be more embarrassing?" Macallan asked her.

"Challenge accepted."

Macallan waved her hands. "Never mind. I give in!"

They both cheered as Ian finished first by a hair. We waited for the official times to be announced. Ian finished in 50.82 — nearly four seconds faster than my best time. And while four seconds doesn't seem like a lot of time, in track it might as well be four hours.

"How do you know Ian?" I asked as Macallan watched him cool down.

"Oh, he came to . . ." She winced.

"He was at the New Year's Eve party," Danielle finished for her. "And he's been asking about Macallan."

"Oh." I guess it shouldn't have surprised me that Macallan would have guys interested in her. And I had a girlfriend, so it would've been completely hypocritical of me to be jealous that she could potentially have a boyfriend.

I told myself I wasn't jealous. Just protective.

Danielle jumped up. "I'm going to get something to drink. And it so happens that I'll need to walk right by Ian. Imagine that."

Macallan groaned. "Have fun — not like I could ever stop you from doing otherwise."

"At least you understand your limitations." Danielle hopped down the bleachers and leaned against the fence as she talked to Ian.

"Is it too late to transfer schools next year?" Macallan asked.

"So, do you like him?" The words came out before I had a chance to stop them.

She shrugged. "I don't know. I don't really know him that well. He's cute."

So he was Macallan's type.

"Well . . ." I didn't know what to say. I knew I should've been supportive about it, but it was making me uneasy. I decided to pretend she was one of my buddies back home. "Why don't you invite him out and we could go on a double date?"

That wince again.

I decided to not dance around this anymore. "Are you in a fight with Emily?" I asked.

"Not exactly." Macallan started digging through her bag. I knew that meant she was avoiding something.

"What's going on, then? You've been acting weird. You're both acting weird." I grabbed her bag so she would stop doing whatever it was she was doing and be forced to pay attention to me.

"I don't want to be stuck in the middle between you two. Just talk to Emily," she stated bluntly.

"I talk to Emily all the time," I reminded her.

"MACALLAN!" Danielle screamed from the track below. "COME SAY HI!"

She groaned. "Look, Levi, I'm in a very awkward position between the two of you and I don't want to have to lie anymore. So talk to Emily. *Really* talk to her."

"What do you mean you don't want to lie to me anymore? Have you been lying?" I'd never thought Macallan was the lying type.

"Not exactly." She grabbed my hand and leaned in. "I'm really sorry. Just talk to Emily."

She hopped up and made her way down to Ian.

I didn't know what bothered me more: the fact that my best friend had been keeping something from me or that she was currently flirting with some guy.

I climbed the steps to Emily's house slowly, feeling the weight of whatever revelation was on the other side of the door.

"Hey!" Emily greeted me with her usual kiss.

"Hey." I tried to smile back at her, but I could tell something was wrong. Something was different. Maybe it had been there for a while, but now I was paying attention.

And so was Emily.

"Is everything okay?" she asked with a tilt of her head, like she was trying to size me up.

"Not really," I confessed. "I think we need to talk."

"Oh." Emily didn't seem surprised. She led me to the couch in the living room. "What's going on?"

"I think you need to tell *me*."

She paused. "I don't know what you're talking about." But that pause told me she knew exactly what I was talking about.

"I talked to Macallan today."

At the mention of Macallan's name, Emily's smile vanished. "And what did Macallan have to say?" There was a sudden hardness in her voice.

"She said you and I needed to talk. She wouldn't say what it was, but it's been pretty clear to me something's been going on. I really wish someone would just tell me. All I know is that it seems Macallan's trying to be a good friend."

"Yeah, some friend," Emily said coldly.

What I wanted to do was stick up for Macallan, who had been best friends with Emily since they were little. I hated that something was getting in the way of their friendship. And that something was me.

I started trying to piece everything together. "Why do I think this doesn't have anything to do with something Macallan did, but something she knows?"

Emily didn't have a response. Which was when I realized I was right.

"Just tell me the truth," I said flatly. I knew in that instant that Emily and I were over. There was no way this was going to involve some kind of misunderstanding that would make everything okay. If it was enough to make Macallan uncomfortable and deceive me, it must've been bad.

Emily studied me briefly before her bottom lip started to tremble. My instincts told me to reach out to her. My head told me this was all an act. I remained still.

"I'm so sorry." She covered her face with her hands. "I'm so sorry." She then leaned into me. I didn't move. I wasn't going to wrap my arms around her and comfort her when she wasn't doing the one thing I'd asked her to do: Tell the truth.

"What happened?"

She straightened up and began wiping away her tears. "I . . ." For a second I thought she wasn't going to tell me. That I would have to get Macallan to fess up.

Emily must've realized she wasn't going to get any sympathy from me. "You know I've been hanging out with Troy. Things just sorta happened on New Year's, but you weren't there, so I didn't think it was a big deal. Then I realized I wanted to see if what he and I had was real, you know? But I didn't want to give up on us and I guess I was confused and didn't know what to do and it's obvious you hate me now."

She finally took a breath, which was enough time for me to understand what she had told me. Something had happened on New Year's Eve. Even though Emily had already told me the opposite. And if I remembered correctly, that was the same time Macallan had started acting different anytime Emily was brought up.

So Macallan knew something had happened and had kept it from me.

I knew I should've been furious with my girlfriend of nearly eight months. But instead I was disappointed in Macallan. She had to choose between Emily and me. And she'd chosen Emily, the liar.

I stood up. "Thanks for telling me the truth at last."

I didn't even wait for a response. I walked out the door and knew there was only one person I wanted to see. I realized I should've been mad at Macallan for keeping this secret from me, but I was more worried that I was going to lose her.

What started as a steady walk quickly developed into a jog. I'd never had to worry about losing a friend over ending a relationship with a girl. But this was different. Macallan had known Emily for practically her entire life. I wasn't going to ask her to take my side, but part of me thought that she was going to be put in that position. I'd be totally cool with her and Emily being friends. But I didn't think Emily was going to be that generous.

While Macallan should've told me what was going on, I didn't really blame her. She was being a good friend to Emily. Because Macallan was a good friend. She was loyal. But that loyalty also made me worried that she would pick Emily.

I could see Macallan in the kitchen when I approached the house. She looked up and saw me. She gave me a weak smile, probably knowing that I finally knew the truth. Or was she dreading having to dump me? She opened the door, and neither of us moved.

"You talked?" she asked.

"Yes."

She nodded. "I'm really sorry I didn't tell you the truth the day you got back. I should've. There's no excuse."

There was this awkwardness between us that we hadn't had since we first met. Neither of us was sure what to do around the other. In that instant, I wished I'd never dated Emily at all. Especially if it had cost me my most important friendship.

"It's not your fault," I said, and noticed her composure relaxed slightly. "We can still be friends, right?" I almost hated how desperate I was for her response, but another part of me didn't care. I'd be lost without Macallan. We both knew that. I'm pretty sure *everybody* knew that.

She looked confused. "Of course."

"You're not going to have to choose?" I felt so juvenile, standing on her front step, begging her to pick me.

"I already did." She stepped aside to let me in.

At first, I felt a little guilty about being responsible for ending Macallan's friendship with Emily. Macallan didn't say much about what happened. It was more like a fact to her: She and Emily were no longer friends.

I wanted to do something to show her how much I appreciated everything she'd done for me. But since I didn't have the means to build her a chef's dream kitchen, I was at a loss. Thankfully, Mom suggested having a joint graduation party with Macallan's family.

And Macallan wasn't allowed to cook. She was going to be pampered that day, all day.

The morning of the ceremony, Mom took her to get a manicure and pedicure. I was invited, but refused — I needed to keep some of my guy points intact. The ceremony was boring. We all got to go up and get a diploma, but we were only graduating eighth grade. We'd see each other that fall, in a different school. With more people. Thankfully.

We headed back to my house afterward. Macallan, her dad and uncle, and me with both my parents and my mom's family from Chicago. Mom had been fretting all week what to make since Macallan had quickly eclipsed Mom's cooking skills.

We all gathered in the living room and snacked on the appetizers (Macallan made sure to compliment Mom's cooking a lot). It wasn't long before Macallan and I broke from the adults and went out to the backyard.

"So does this mean we're officially young adults now?" I asked her.

"I don't know. I've already been reading those kinds of books for a few years."

"Uh-oh, does this mean I'm still a baby? I really love *Everyone Poops*."

"Do you need me to answer that?" She nudged me playfully.

"Probably not."

Silence fell between us. This was a common occurrence whenever we're alone. When you're comfortable with someone, you don't need to always fill the void with noise. I liked it when we would just be.

"Do you think next year will be different?" Macallan asked.

"I don't know. I'm excited about it, though, you know?"

She shrugged. "I guess."

I could tell she was uneasy about the move. It made sense. What was strange was that I wasn't that nervous. I was excited. I felt the new school would give me another start. More opportunities.

"Everything could change," she said in a quiet voice before she shot me a look. "Or not. Blimey if I have a clue."

"Hey, that's my line," I teased before I put my arm around her. "Listen, nothing will change with us. I promise you right here, right now, that I'll be there for you through good times, bad times, friend issues, boy issues, teacher issues, whatever issues. And you'll always have a date to any social event that requires a male companion. I hear I clean up nicely."

"I wouldn't trust your sources." A smile was now on her lips. "And what makes you think I couldn't get my own date?"

I shook my head at her. "For the record, I don't think you'd have a problem finding a date. I just imagine every guy will pale in comparison to me and never live up to your clearly heightened expectations."

She looked at me flatly. "The only thing heightened around here is your ego."

"Fine, fine. I'll go stag, then." I dropped my head.

"Okay, fine. If neither of us has a date, we should do things like homecoming together. Why not? Everybody thinks we're a couple anyway."

"Why not? I guess I'll take that as a yes. Sound good?" I held out my hand.

She shook it. "Sounds perfect."

It was kinda perfect. And you didn't seem *that* horrified when I took you to homecoming freshman year.

> That was fun. Freshman year was really great, actually. Pretty easy transition. We both made some new friends. No emotional trauma that wasn't solved with a *Buggy and Floyd* marathon.

And then you had to get a boyfriend.

> It was only a matter of time before I was snatched up, especially when you can bake a brownie like I do.

Oh, is that what the kids are calling it these days? *Baking brownies?*

> Gross. But don't forget that *you* got a girlfriend at the start of sophomore year.

Yes, I did.

> But did the questions stop about whether or not we were a couple?

No, they did not.

CHAPTER NINE

If I could've talked to my eighth-grade self, I would've told her she had nothing to worry about. Freshman year was easy. Admittedly, having a boyfriend who'd already spent a year there helped a lot.

"Are you cold?" Ian put his arm around me.

"Why do I have a feeling that was just an excuse to get closer to me?" I leaned into him.

He gave me a little squeeze as we sat in the bleachers during the JV football game at the beginning of sophomore year. Of course, Ian had assumed Levi and I were dating when high school first started. I couldn't really blame him. Not only did Levi and I go to and leave school together (unless he had practice), we sat together at lunch, went to homecoming together, and did pretty much everything together.

I got it. I really did. But that still didn't mean I was going to stop spending time with my best friend.

I guess Ian figured it out because he asked me on a date the Saturday after Thanksgiving. By the time the JV game came along, we'd been together for ten months, and not once had he ever complained about Levi to me. Sure, he'd tease me, but I knew I deserved most of it.

"Have I ever told you that you're too good a friend?" Ian laughed.

"There's always a chance that he'll get in." I hoped the universe heard me on that one.

We were at the football game to support Levi, even though he'd never made it to the field. Ever. Not as a freshman, not during the first two games of sophomore year. It wasn't the running he struggled with; the coach repeatedly told him he was the fastest on the team. It was catching the ball that was the issue.

So Levi sat on the bench. But he was a part of a team.

And Levi was a part of my life, which is why I was also sitting on a bench.

"Do I need to remind you that I come to all your track meets in the spring?" I nudged Ian.

"Do *I* need to remind *you* that Levi's also competing? So let's not pretend you're there just for me."

I opened my mouth in shock. "Exactly what are you implying?"

He shook his head. "Nothing. I'm certainly not questioning your allegiances. I know I'd lose that battle. Plus, you know I like him . . . except for the fact that he's getting close to beating my times."

I hid my face. I was grateful that the only time my boyfriend and best friend got competitive was during track. The varsity track coach, Mr. Scharfenberg, had already told Levi he was pretty much a shoo-in to be on the varsity team this year.

Ian and I sat through the entire game. I tried to pretend to be interested in what was going on, but honestly, if Levi wasn't playing or the players weren't wearing green and gold, I couldn't have cared less.

I did spend a significant amount of time avoiding eye contact with the cheerleaders. Emily performed like she didn't have a care in the world, and she probably didn't. She'd dated Troy for a bit, followed by Keith, then James, then Mark, then Dave. Despite all her concerns, she never struggled to fit in. She had an even bigger circle of friends now.

Danielle had gone with me "in the divorce," which was good, because I'd really needed her dry sense of humor to help me after the breakup. Whenever Emily and I had class together, we'd sit and chat, but as soon as the bell rang, she'd go to her new friends. But I had new friends of my own, which made it easier not to have hard feelings.

After the game was over, Ian and I waited by the locker room for Levi.

He exited the building with a gray hoodie pulled low over his head. His entire posture showed defeat.

"Hi!" I tried to be enthusiastic for him, but not too enthusiastic.

"Hey, guys." Levi continued to look down at the floor.

"I told your mom we'd give you a ride home. But first maybe some custard? On Ian?"

"Hey!" Ian grabbed me by the waist.

I swatted his hands away. "Ever the gentleman."

Levi wasn't amused. "Nah, I'm okay." He wouldn't even look at us.

There were two words for a moment like this: *awk-ward*.

We got into Ian's car. I could practically feel Levi's eyes roll into the back of his head when a rap song came blasting from the stereo. I turned the music down.

"So, Levi." Ian glanced in the rearview mirror. "I heard you're dating Carrie Pope?"

I didn't think you could technically call one coffee and one movie *dating*. But Levi nodded.

"Isn't she a freshman?" Ian's interest in Levi's dating life was making me anxious.

"Hey, pot, are you calling this kettle black?" Levi said with a laugh. I was relieved that he still had his sense of humor.

"No," Ian stammered. "I'm just saying she's cute."

"Hey!" I playfully hit his arm.

"That's not what I meant. She's not my type."

"Oh, so cute isn't your type?" I countered.

"Sounded like that to me," Levi announced from the backseat.

"You know, you guys are no fun," Ian sulked. "Nobody can ever win anything with the two of you ganging up on poor, poor souls."

"Oh, please." I turned around and gave Levi a high five just to annoy Ian further.

"Blimey if we can help it," Levi said in a British accent.

"Ack!" Ian protested. "Enough with that blimey stuff. You guys are too much."

"I believe he means too much awesome," I clarified.

"Clearly," Levi agreed. "Can't imagine what else it would be."

"Unless it's amazing."

"That's another word people often use to describe us."

"And fabulous," I reminded him.

"Inspiring."

"Extraordinary."

"Stop!" Ian cried out like he was in physical pain. "Oh, I've got plenty of words to describe you two. Believe me."

He pulled over in front of Levi's house. "So, Levi, how about we even the playing field and go on a double date. Then maybe Carrie and I can gang up on you two for a change."

An odd silence took over the car. Levi and I were no longer joking around. I don't know why we were both reacting so strangely. It wasn't as if Levi didn't hang out with us, but now we were adding a fourth. Would it be uncomfortable?

"Was it something I said?" Ian asked, to lighten the mood.

I tried to grasp on to reality and not overreact. "No, yeah, I think that would be great."

I looked at Levi, who was studying my face. "Sure," he said. Although he didn't sound sure.

"Great!" Ian was way too excited about this. "We've got that party at Keith's next weekend."

"We do?" I hadn't known *we* had that.

"Yeah, didn't I tell you?" I shook my head in response. He continued. "Oh, well, let's go grab a bite beforehand and go over together."

"Ah, okay." Levi got out of the car and gave me a little wave before going inside.

"See." Ian leaned over toward me. "Look at me playing nice with your BFF. What does this get me?"

"The privilege of driving me home," I stated flatly.

He laughed. "You're something else. You know that, right?"

So I've been told.

I didn't know if it should comfort me that Levi was as hesitant about the double date as I was. I'd met Carrie a couple of times, but I'd tried to give her lots of space. I knew that Levi having a girl as a best friend could be intimidating. She seemed sweet and he liked her, so I wanted it to work for him.

Plus, I had learned to knock before entering rooms, both literally and metaphorically.

The four of us were eerily quiet on the drive over to the restaurant for Friday night fish fry. I gave Levi the front seat, thinking he and Ian could talk about guy things and I could get to know Carrie more.

"I like your skirt," I offered. Carrie was wearing an orange skirt with an off-white cashmere wrap sweater.

"Thanks. I like your outfit, too," she replied, although I was only wearing jeans and a basic black top. But she was clearly trying to make an effort.

"Thanks."

She smiled at me. "And you have, like, the best hair." She started fiddling with her own long honey-brown hair.

"You've got great hair, too."

She shrugged her shoulders. "My color is so boring."

Levi turned around. "Seriously, hair and clothing? Way to shatter stereotypes, Macallan."

I shot him my patented death stare. "What were you guys going to talk about, sports?"

"Well, we're clearly manly."

"Seriously? You want me to get in this with you right now in front of Carrie." I raised my eyebrow, daring him.

He turned back around. "I knew this was a bad idea."

While I was pretty sure he was saying it in a joking manner, I agreed with him one hundred percent.

I tried to adjust my attitude as we sat down at Curran's Tavern. We made small talk before the waiter came over and took our orders.

Levi gave me a crooked smile. "Shall I order or do you want to?"

"We always get the same thing," I explained to our confused companions. "Yes, I'll have the fried cod with baked potato, but can I please have extra sour cream with that? And blue cheese dressing on the salad. Thanks."

"I'll have what she's having," Levi announced. "Although you forgot one thing."

"Oh! Cheese curds!" I practically screamed. "Um, can we start with an order of fried cheese curds as well? Thanks."

The waiter nodded and turned toward Carrie, who asked for a grilled chicken Caesar salad.

"And I'll have the cheeseburger, medium rare," Ian ordered.

I didn't have to say anything, because I knew Levi would.

"Seriously? Who goes to a fish fry and doesn't get fish?" He shook his head. "First of all, I will not be sharing my corn fritters with either of you, and I know for a fact that Macallan won't, either."

"Preach it," I encouraged.

Levi leaned in, his face so serious it was almost solemn. "Listen, guys, I never heard of a Friday night fish fry until Macallan's family took my family. You have no idea how spoiled you are in Wisconsin: fried fish, corn fritters with honey butter, baked beans, bread and butter, coleslaw, potatoes — you get your choice of potato! And did I mention the butter? So much butter! I mean, what more could you want on a Friday night? Ordering something else . . . It's madness, madness, I say!"

While Carrie and Ian didn't look as amused as I was, a strange sense of pride overwhelmed me. If only seventh-grade Levi could see himself now. He was even starting to get a little Midwestern accent.

"What are you smiling at?" Levi inquired.

"Nothing," I responded a little too quickly.

"Like I would ever fall for that." He leaned forward and gazed in my eyes as if he was trying to read my mind. I looked away. At that point, I wouldn't have doubted that he could. "Ah, see, I know you're up to something."

"Who, me?" I said in my most innocent voice.

"Please." He leaned back and put his arm around the back of Carrie's chair. "Let me tell you a little something about this one, Carrie. Do not fall for the good-girl, straight-A-student façade. Beneath her sweet exterior is a snarky center with quick wit and even quicker rebounds."

"Which is exactly why you're best friends with me."

"Obviously," Levi agreed.

Ian cleared his voice loudly. "So, Carrie, I think we need to intervene before the *Levi and Macallan Show* takes over. Once they get started, they don't stop. Ever."

Carrie maneuvered uncomfortably in her chair and played with her straw wrapper.

I mouthed *sorry* to Ian. This wasn't the first time, nor did I think it would be the last, he'd had to intervene when Levi and I got into one of our epic conversations.

I ended up playing twenty get-to-know-you questions with Carrie until our food arrived. Besides being really sweet, she was running for student council and volunteering at the animal shelter on the weekends. I felt like a total slacker in comparison.

Although I was having a good time, I had to fight every instinct I had to talk to Levi whenever a thought came up that I knew he'd enjoy or have a comeback for. I needed to be on my best behavior. We had our dates to consider. After all, it was a pretty big miracle we could find members of the opposite sex who enjoyed our company as much as we did.

We arrived at Keith's house when the party was in full swing. Everybody from the football team, cheerleading squad, and marching band was there.

"Hey, California!" Keith came over and did that guy hand-slap/chest-bump combination that must be taught in some dude class. "Welcome, welcome, all!" He looked me up and down, and I gave him a stare that made it clear I wasn't the least bit interested in anything he was looking for.

"Hey, man," Ian said, coming between us. "Thanks for the invite."

"Oh, right, you two are together. See, I keep forgetting that, since she's always with him." He pointed to a clearly annoyed Levi.

"Keith, this is Carrie." Levi gestured in her direction.

For whatever reason, Keith laughed. "Okay, I get it, I get it." He reached down in a cooler and pulled out some cans of pop. "I'd say go long, Levi, but I don't think my mom would appreciate getting pop on the carpet." He laughed again. We all remained stone-faced.

We each took a can and made our way over to the corner of the kitchen.

"Don't let him get to you," I said to Levi.

"But he's right. I can't catch anything . . . except grief." He shook his head.

I turned my back to Carrie and Ian. I knew how embarrassed Levi got about his lack of catching skills. "You're getting much better. The other day, Adam was telling me you caught a ball nearly all the way down the block."

"I guess." His voice was faint. "But it's so humiliating sitting on that bench every single game."

"I thought you only wanted to play football to make some friends and fit in."

He shrugged. "But it doesn't mean I don't want to play."

"I know, but look around. You're at a party and Keith invited you."

"He invited *everybody*."

"But at least you're here. And he's ribbing you. Isn't that the bro way of being friendly?"

"The bro way." He laughed.

"You know, how guys show affection. Or mark their turf. Kind of like how dogs pee on something to let you know it's theirs."

"Do you have any idea of what you're talking about?"

"Of course not," I admitted. "But does it at least make you feel a little better?"

"Yeah, just a little."

I elbowed him playfully. "Well, that will not do. Clearly my job here is not done. Let me count the ways that you're a stud."

"Wait, wait." Levi pulled out his phone. "I need to record this. I may even make it my ringtone."

I grabbed his phone and spoke directly into the mic. "I, Macallan Marion Dietz, do hereby swear that Levi Rodgers is a total manly man, the ultimate bro. Reason number one, he does a mean British accent. Reason number two, he knows to always compliment a lady's cooking skills. Um, reason number three. Um . . ."

"Nice." He grabbed his phone back. "You can't even come up with three reasons?"

"See, there are just so many reasons, my poor brain is on overload."

"Good save."

"Phew!" I wiped my brow dramatically.

"Hey!" Danielle approached us. "I didn't see you guys come

in. But then I saw your dates outside and figured you were doing that thing you do."

Danielle could read the nonverbal exchange Levi and I shared. "Let me guess. You didn't realize your dates left."

I grimaced.

She shook her head. "You guys are too much."

"Clearly," Levi and I said in unison.

"Well, may I suggest that you take your party outside and keep your dates company?"

"Thanks!" I gave Danielle a quick hug before she returned to her marching band friends.

Levi and I went to the glass patio door and saw Carrie and Ian leaning against the deck railing. Ian was telling some story that was making Carrie laugh.

"Well, at least they're having a good time," Levi remarked. "In fact, it looks like they're having a better time now than they did at dinner."

"Levi." I stopped him from opening the door. "I think that maybe it's not the best idea for us to go on double dates."

He nodded. "I know. It's hard to throw anybody into our mix. I don't want to mess things up with Carrie."

"You and I will still hang out. I'm only saying that maybe date night should just be date night. Not forcing our dates to put up with the two of us."

Levi's gaze was fixed straight ahead. His jaw was tightly clenched.

"Levi?"

When he didn't respond, I followed his stare. Ian moved closer to Carrie and tucked a piece of hair behind her ear.

She blushed, but leaned into him. He then put his arm around her.

"Are they *flirting*?" I gasped out. There was no way this was happening.

Levi and I remained frozen as we watched Ian and Carrie get closer and closer. He said something else that made her laugh. She twirled a piece of hair with her finger. Then he leaned farther into her. Her smile dropped. They were studying each other. Intensely.

I recognized that look on Ian. He tilted his head and put his index finger up to her chin.

This was so not happening.

"I can't . . ." Levi's pained voice snapped me into action.

I slid the glass door so quickly it rattled.

"How could you?" I found myself in front of Carrie. I know I should've been more upset with Ian, but at that moment I was furious at Carrie. Levi had been on a few dates with her, he'd asked her to come hang out with his friends and go to a party he was invited to, and *this* was how she repaid him?

Carrie shrank from me. But Ian stepped closer. "Are you being serious right now?" I'd never seen him mad before. But he was mad now.

"Are *you* being serious right now?" I threw back.

He looked at me with disgust. "Do you realize how messed up this is? You're mad at Carrie? Do you even care about me? You know what — you don't need to answer that. It's clear that your only concern is Levi, not your boyfriend. No, wait, your *former* boyfriend."

"Let me make sure I'm getting this straight." My mind

was trying to keep up with everything that had happened in the past few minutes. "*You* were flirting with another girl. If I hadn't stepped in, *you* were probably going to kiss another girl. *You* were going to cheat on me. Yet *you're* mad at *me*? And *you're* breaking up with *me*?"

"Do you have any idea how much this hurts me?" Ian's voice cracked, and I could tell it was completely genuine. I felt awful. Maybe I had hurt him. But I certainly knew I didn't do anything that justified cheating.

"How are you putting this on me?" Confusion swirled around in my head. Ian and I had never fought. Not once. We were talking about going into Milwaukee for our one-year anniversary. And now he was breaking up with me? "Have you been drinking?"

"You know I don't drink," he snapped at me. "Maybe I did do this on purpose, for you to see what it's like to have your boyfriend give another girl all your attention. I really like you, Macallan. But I can't sit here and play second best to Levi anymore."

"You wouldn't think any of this if he was a girl."

"But he's not. And that's the problem. Why don't you two just go out already?"

This was what it always came down to. The perception that there was no way Levi and I could be legitimately best friends and only friends. Nobody ever got that.

Mostly because those people never had a best friend of the opposite sex.

Or maybe it would be more appropriate to say that none of those people had Levi as a best friend.

"If you've had such a problem with it, why are you only saying something now?"

He groaned. "Because I figured that the closer you and I got, the less I'd have to deal with him?"

"Deal with him?"

"You know what I mean."

"No, I don't."

I nearly jumped out of my skin when I heard Levi's voice say, "I'm so sorry." I had forgotten that he and Carrie were there. In fact, a whole crowd had started gathering around the door.

Carrie was hunched over in a clear attempt to disappear. "I should go," she said quietly.

"I'll drive you home." Ian walked into the group of observers with Carrie following behind him.

I heard some clapping. "Dudes," Keith called out, emerging from the crowd. "I know I can always count on you two for entertainment. If only I had some popcorn! That was insane."

"Really, Keith?" I asked.

Something in my voice stopped him. "Oh, man, I'm sorry, Macallan."

I stood there waiting for him to make a sarcastic follow-up comment. But he had a look of actual sympathy on his face. Which made me feel even worse. If Keith felt bad for you, you knew your life must be pathetic.

"Let's get out of here." I grabbed Levi by the arm and led us out of the house.

"Um, our ride left," Levi said with quiet resignation.

"We'll figure something out." I opened the door and started walking. "I think fresh air might do us some good."

Levi stayed uncharacteristically silent for several minutes. I left him alone with his thoughts, as I had a ton of mine to sort out. Mostly, what had just happened? Maybe I was missing some signals. I racked my brain for signs that Ian had been unhappy. He'd made lots of jabs at how much time I spent with Levi and usually pretended to gag whenever I would talk about him. But he was a guy. I'd thought he was teasing me.

Regardless of what I'd done, it didn't give him any excuse to flirt the second my back was turned. But what made me the most upset was that it had been Levi's girlfriend. I would've thought Ian would've wanted Levi to have a girlfriend.

"Is any of this making sense to you?" I asked Levi.

He shook his head and kept walking. This was bad.

We found ourselves walking to the same place. We didn't discuss where we were going, we just led each other to Riverside Park. We silently walked over to the swing set and sat down. Me in the middle swing with Levi seated to my left. This was how we always sat when we'd go to the park after school in seventh grade.

I started rocking my swing back and forth.

"So I've been thinking," Levi announced, remaining motionless on his swing. "I think you're right. We shouldn't go on any more double dates."

I looked over and saw a slight smile on his face. "Are you making a joke?"

"Well, it's either that or come to face the fact that I've been cheated on twice."

"She didn't technically cheat."

He clicked his tongue. "Yeah, only because you stopped it."

"We don't know what was going to happen." I didn't believe the words as they came out of my mouth. I tried to lighten the mood. "I guess I really need to stop going to parties where your girlfriends are. And where there are doors."

"Tell me about it."

He got up and went behind to push me. I closed my eyes and let the swing take me higher and higher.

We stayed like that for nearly an hour. I glanced down at my watch. "We either have to start walking home or call one of our parents."

We decided it was best to call Levi's mom for the ride. Dad and Uncle Adam were very protective of me, so I didn't think they would take it lightly that I'd been essentially abandoned at a party. Although I *was* with Levi, which would've made them feel a little bit better. They both really liked Ian, so I knew they'd be disappointed to hear it was over.

Over. It was so strange to think about it.

Levi and I sat on the curb while we waited for his mom.

"Are you okay?" I asked.

"Not really." He wrapped his arms around his legs. "I don't know, I'm wondering if there's something wrong with me."

"There's nothing wrong with you," I assured him.

"But why do girls keep cheating on me?"

"You've had one girl cheat on you and one girl make a poor decision."

He sighed. "Maybe I'm a bad kisser."

"I'm sure it's not that."

"How would you know?" He got me there. "Let's think about it. My first girlfriend here was away from me for ten days and started sucking face with some other guy the second she was alone with him. Tonight my girlfriend was away from me for like two seconds and she was going to make out with another guy. It clearly has to be me."

"You're being silly."

"I don't think I am." Then Levi was the opposite of quiet. He spent the next five minutes going on and on about how it must be that he was a horrible kisser and that he would never have a girlfriend because he's lousy. How he was never going to date another girl because he couldn't trust them. How pathetic he must be that EVERY girl jumped at the chance to be with someone the second his back was turned.

It was getting extremely annoying.

Levi was usually pretty laid back about things, so I wasn't used to his being so hard on himself over a girl. And being so overdramatic.

I kept trying to tell him it wasn't about him. It was about how Emily liked to flirt and wasn't really "girlfriend material" because she preferred to date and play the field. And who knew about Carrie? She was young. She'd made a mistake.

But that wasn't enough. I was getting so frustrated with Levi. Part of me wanted to smack him, but I knew that wouldn't shut him up.

"Nope, that's it. I'm a horrible kisser. And it's going to spread around school and then no girl will ever give me a chance."

"For the love, Levi!" I shouted at him.

And before I really knew what I was doing, I grabbed his cheeks and pulled him in for a kiss. He was tense, probably from shock, for the first couple seconds. Then his arms were around me and he eased into it.

I pulled away and Levi struggled for breath. "Wh-wh-what . . ." he stammered.

"You're fine. You are not a bad kisser. It has been verified. Moving on."

His eyes were wide, his mouth speechless.

I loved that he was so flustered.

We saw his mom's car approaching. I stood up and he remained on the curb. I reached out my hand to help him up. It took him a second to process it. He got up on his feet, still completely stunned.

"So that's one thing I have over your friends in California and your bros here," I said to him.

He returned a blank stare.

I laughed and hit him on the shoulder. "I don't think any of them would've had the nerve to prove to you that you're not a bad kisser. You're welcome, by the way."

He stayed mostly silent for the ride to my house.

I laughed silently to myself in the backseat.

All it really takes to fluster a guy is a simple kiss.

Yeah.

Still speechless, I see?

Give me a break, will you? There I was, pouring my heart out, when you *attacked* me. I usually prefer to be taken out on a date first. At least buy a guy a slice of pizza before you take advantage of him. Especially if he's emotionally fragile.

Yes, poor you. You were being ridiculous and that was the only thing I could think to do to shut you up.

I really need to start talking more.

Are you blushing?

Um, what were we talking about?

How I'm the love of your life.

Obviously.

CHAPTER TEN

Here's the basic difference between having a girl as a best friend as opposed to a guy.

When you complain incessantly to your guy friends about being cheated on and how you might not be a good kisser, they'll give you crap, change the subject, or even smack you.

But when you're best friends with a girl and you blather on and on, she kisses you to make you shut up.

When it first happened, I was shocked and confused for the first 1.3 seconds. Then I decided to go with it. Macallan was an *excellent* kisser. I was a little disappointed when she pulled away and acted like nothing had happened.

And people think guys don't get attached when things get physical.

Of course, I tried to get her to kiss me again. But she didn't fall for it. Anytime I'd be purposely annoying to her, I'd say, "Uh-oh, somebody better get me to shut up," and then pucker my lips. Macallan would ignore me and go back to whatever she was doing.

That was annoying.

IIIIIIIIIIIIIIIIIIIIIIIIIIIIIIIIIIIIIIIIII

Spring finally arrived, and with it came the warmer weather and track.

Even though we were already in the middle of the season, I still got nervous for every race. It mattered too much to me. I had to keep telling myself to remember to breathe. Then I shook my legs out. I could hear the introductions and the crowd. But I looked straight ahead. The only thing that mattered was the 400 meters in front of me.

I heard the call to line up. I positioned myself at the start, ready to bound forward at the sound of the shot.

I went into this zone right before a race. Everything else faded away; I gained tunnel vision. A calmness overcame me as my body readied itself to pounce, to run.

The shot rang and I blasted out. My muscles automatically responded from all the training I'd done. I breathed in short bursts, propelling my body faster and faster. I rounded the first bend of the track and could sense that we were in a tight group. By the halfway mark, I knew there were only a couple other runners left. I used every ounce of energy for the remaining course, not wanting to leave anything behind.

I knew it must've been close because the only voice I could hear was Macallan's, and she was being more intense than usual. When I crossed the finish line, it took me several yards to get down to a jog. I looked next to me and Ian was right by my side.

"It's gonna be a tight one, man." He gasped, clearly out of breath.

I could only nod. I hadn't yet fully recovered.

He patted me on my back.

Ian and I had formed a sort of truce after the near-cheating incident. I was more upset with him for what he'd done to Macallan, though she didn't seem as bothered by it as I would've been. But I guessed that when you've been through everything she had, breaking up with a boyfriend in high school wasn't the worst loss.

"Branigan, Rodgers, good job!" Coach Scharfenberg called to us as we slowly made our way back to the team.

The coaches and officials spent a few minutes going over the official times.

"Hey, you coming out after?" Ian asked me.

"Yeah." The guys on the varsity team always went out after the meets. It usually involved a lot of food and Gatorade.

"Awesome job!" Andy handed me some water.

"Thanks, you killed it in the two hundred."

"Totally." Tim came up and patted Andy on the back. "Although let's face it, I smoked the relay. As I do."

I actually had guy friends. Like, real guy friends. Once I'd made varsity (the only sophomore to do so), I'd started hanging out with Tim and Andy, both juniors. They were these cool guys who were really supportive. I would just relax and try not to get too giddy whenever they'd ask me to do stuff.

I did have to break plans with Macallan a few times, but I knew she was happy for me. Plus, she always planned everything way in advance, which these guys didn't.

I stared at the scoreboard, willing the times to be posted. And it *was* close.

Ian had beaten me by one-tenth of a second.

One-tenth.

In some ways, I would rather have lost by a second. Races this close always haunted me. I didn't think I had anything left in me, but

I couldn't help but think if I'd only pushed myself a little faster, only two-tenths faster, I would've won.

"Good job, man!" Ian patted me on the back.

"Congrats — you earned it."

I went over to the side where Macallan and Danielle were waiting.

"Hey." I tried to smile.

"You were great!" Macallan exclaimed, and gave me a big hug. I felt so embarrassed because not only had I lost, but I was covered in sweat.

I shrugged, not willing to accept the compliment. Especially when it wasn't warranted.

"Come on — you're a sophomore," she reminded me. "Second place is amazing. You'll totally get it next time."

Yeah, when Ian was no longer on the team.

Macallan grabbed my shoulders and started shaking me. "Earth to Levi! You were incredible. We're going to Culver's — frozen custard on me!"

"As much as I'd love to see you open your wallet for a change, I'm going out with the guys." I playfully messed up her hair.

She swatted my hand away. "Oh, right, guy time. Manly time. Bro time. Oh, wait, is that a smile I see?" She scrunched up her face and pretended she was searching for clues in my face. "Yep, there's definitely a smile cracking. You know what will probably get a huge grin is quality time spent around dudes. Yep, *manly men*, doing *manly things*."

"Too bad," Danielle joined in. "Macallan and I were going to have a lingerie pillow fight."

"Totally." Macallan's eyebrows went up and down. "And to think, there was something else I was going to do. I don't know, it was on the edge of my lips." She playfully puckered her lips and tapped them. "Hmm, don't know what it was."

"You're awful." I desperately tried to get the thought of Macallan and Danielle in lingerie out of my mind. That was up-and-down cruel. I sometimes thought Macallan forgot I was a guy. And we have certain responses that are difficult to control.

"I'm only teasing." She bumped her hip against mine.

Yes, *tease* was the appropriate word.

"I've got to hit the showers." A very, very cold shower.

"Have fun tonight. Really." She gave me another big hug. Which didn't help my current situation. "I'm proud of you and I'll see you tomorrow. Now go have fun with the boys."

"Yes, be super manly," Danielle said.

They both laughed and walked away.

"Dude." Andy followed me into the locker room. "There's no way I can ask her to prom, even if I promise to be a gentleman?"

I shook my head. No way.

"It's pretty cruel that you parade her around me, but it's all look, don't touch."

Join the club, I thought.

Tim and Andy had been working with me on my catching skills. Even Keith had joined us a few times and thought I could play, actually play, on the varsity team the next year.

This was the life I'd dreamed of when we drove to Wisconsin four years ago. Being with a crew, being popular. I didn't care how shallow it sounded. It was true.

I walked to classes in a group. I hung out with a group. *My* group. Girls were paying more attention to me.

It was about two weeks after Macallan and I had shared that sweaty hug when I was with my crew at our after-meet dinner.

"California!" Andy started slamming his hands against the table.

Tim joined him with his fists banging. "California, come on!" Soon the entire table was chanting my nickname.

I picked up the milk shake and chugged the entire thing. I didn't care that I could hardly taste it or that the cold burned my throat. My guys were cheering me on.

"Dude!" Andy laughed. "That was insane. Twenty-six seconds. You totally crushed Tim's time."

"Won't be the last time that happens," I boasted, ignoring the instant pounding in my head from brain freeze.

Andy straightened up a bit and ran his hands quickly over his hair. He then jutted his chin out. "What's up, Macallan?"

I turned around to see that Macallan had walked in with Danielle. They took a corner table.

"Dude, come on," Andy pleaded. "Ask her to join us."

I couldn't tell if the lurch I felt was from slamming a milk shake or Andy's constant insistence on being set up with Macallan.

Andy took my silence as a non-invitation for Macallan to join us. He seemed to concede . . . but then he popped out of his seat and headed over to her table.

I could only see part of Macallan's face as Andy approached. She looked confused at first, then gave him a big grin. Andy said something that made her laugh and I jumped up.

"What's going on?" I put my arm around Andy and gave Macallan an apologetic look. "Is he bothering you?"

"I'm inviting these lovely ladies over to our table." Andy bowed his head.

Danielle picked up her menu and refused to look up. Her tolerance for "stupid boy shenanigans" was about as high as Macallan's.

I knew the only way to get Andy to leave was to make him jealous.

"Hey, you." I pushed Andy aside and sat down next to Macallan. "What are you getting?" I rested my chin on her shoulder for extra effect. "Let me guess, tuna melt?"

"Maybe . . ." I saw her give Danielle a look that resulted in a conspiratorial smirk.

Quiet settled on the table. Andy excused himself, but I wanted to wait a few more minutes just to make a point that nobody else was allowed to be at this table.

"I'm going to go wash my hands." Danielle got up and left.

I moved over to her side of the booth. "So what's going on?"

Macallan shrugged. "Not much. Are you coming to Sunday night supper?"

"I can't — I've got something at Keith's. But Mom and Dad are still coming."

She looked down at the menu again. This place had only about three things she would eat, so I didn't know why she needed to study it so much.

"Oh, also, I can't do Wednesday, either. I've got —"

"Something with the guys," she talked over me, a bitter edge seeping into her voice.

"Ah, yeah." I took her menu away. "Look, I'm sorry I've been preoccupied."

"I get it." I could tell she was hurt. She was used to me not having any plans. I couldn't help it if the guys had me booked. I was a man in demand. "So will you be able to come to Adam's birthday party?"

"Isn't that months away?"

"Well, thought I'd get you to commit now. Even if you'll probably cancel at the last minute."

I decided to ignore the passive-aggressive comment.

Macallan picked up her soda and took a long sip. She paused for a second, then put the soda down and said, "So Keith asked me out again."

"He did what?" I blurted loudly.

"Yeah, he came up to me yesterday after class." She folded her body over like she was a caveman. "*You. Me. Date. Grunt.* I said no. Obviously."

"Why didn't you tell me?"

She studied my face. "I texted you yesterday to call me, but alas, you didn't get back to me. Shocking." Her lips were pursed. I remembered getting her text, but it had been during practice. And while I shouldn't have ignored her, she'd been sending a lot more texts than normal lately. It bordered on needy. "Besides, I would've thought he told you."

"No, he didn't. He knew I wouldn't be okay with that. I've made it clear that you're off-limits."

"I'm *off-limits*?" she snapped. "What does *that* mean?"

"It's just, like, you know . . ."

"No, I don't know." She pulled the elastic out of her hair and immediately put her hair up again, her hands working quickly. I could tell she was annoyed. She needed something to give her a few seconds to figure out what to say next. "You're such a hypocrite."

I wasn't expecting that.

Disgust filled her voice. "It's totally okay for you to get a whole group of guy friends, but heaven forbid one of them wants to go out with me."

She had completely lost me. "You *want* to go out with Keith?"

"No! This isn't about Keith." She looked down at the table. "Well, at least someone in your group wants to spend time with me."

This wasn't like Macallan. She wasn't the kind of person who felt sorry for herself.

"Do you want me to go over there" — I pointed to my table — "and tell them I won't hang out with them anymore. Is that what you want?"

That familiar cold look started to creep over her face. "You know I don't want that. And I'm sorry I want to spend some time with you."

"Well, we've got the summer."

"That feels like it's ages from now."

I saw Danielle approaching and got up. "But seriously, if you *want* to go out with Keith . . ."

She grimaced.

"Oi!" I called out, knowing how to temper this situation. "Blimey if he don't fancy him a sweetheart. Before ya know it, he'll be bringing 'round roses and Bob's your uncle."

I waited for her to reply. She sat there stubbornly for a few moments before she responded in a monotone, "But, Buggy, you're uncle's name is Sam."

I quickly turned on my heel. I figured it was best for me to leave her quoting *Buggy and Floyd* than to get in a fight.

Macallan and I didn't really fight. It wasn't our thing.

But this felt like a fight.

IIIIIIIIIIIIIIIIIIIIIIIIIIIIIIIIIIIIIIIIIIII

I was so busy with track, practicing ball, and studying for finals as our sophomore year came to an end. But I made a note to spend at least an entire day with Macallan as soon as school was over.

Now we had only one more day to go and then we'd be free.

As much as I loved my guys, I had started to miss Macallan. When I was with her, I didn't have to always be on. Sure, she and I would trade barbs, but she was also the only person I could have a real conversation with. I thought if I got too deep with the guys, they'd think I was turning into a girl.

"Hey, you." Macallan came up to me after school with Danielle not far behind. "I've been texting you all week."

"Hey!" I started shoving books in my backpack.

"Are you —"

"Rodgers!" Tim boomed. "You're so going to pay for that stunt in gym."

"Good luck with that!" I shouted back. I turned back to Macallan. "Sorry. What were you saying?"

She looked flustered. "I was wondering —"

"CATCH!" I heard Keith call out. I turned around and perfectly caught the football he'd thrown.

"Mr. Simon, no throwing in the halls," a teacher reprimanded him.

"Sorry! Sorry!" Keith played bashful, until the teacher turned her back. "Nice work, California! We've got all summer to throw the pigskin around."

"I hear that." We high-fived.

I finally realized Macallan was trying to tell me something. I looked around and couldn't find her. I saw Danielle up the hallway and went after her.

"Yo!" I called out.

She turned around and gave me a death stare.

"*Yo*? You've *got* to be kidding me." She kept walking.

"Where's Macallan?"

"Oh, so you noticed her existence?" she said dryly.

"Come on, I —"

She interrupted me. "No, totally, *dude*. I get it. You had your *bros* around. Chillax, yo."

Wow. A girl was overreacting. Paging Captain Cliché.

"Try her locker," she said over her shoulder.

I raced to Macallan's locker. And was relieved to see her, until she turned around and looked like she was about to cry.

I'd only seen Macallan cry about her mom. She handled everything else — the dissolving of her friendship with Emily, her breakup with Ian, academic stress — with this quiet strength.

"Hey, hey!" I ran up to her, but she began walking in the opposite direction. "You're mad at me?"

She didn't need to answer when she turned around. The look on her face said enough. But unfortunately, she answered, "What do you think?"

"I'm sorry." Even though I had no idea what had gotten her so mad. I'd only been fooling around with my friends at my locker. She couldn't have waited a minute or two before she would have had my undivided attention? Of course she couldn't. She was used to having me all to herself.

But now I had other friends, other commitments.

It wasn't my problem if she couldn't handle that.

She laughed. "You know, I usually believe you when you apologize, but I have a feeling you have no idea what this is about."

"Actually I do."

"Oh, really? Would you care to enlighten me?" She was being so smug, it made me even angrier.

"You don't like that your little errand and whipping boy isn't at your beck and call."

She stared blankly at me. I'd got her so good.

"No." Her voice was so quiet. "It's that I think I'm losing my best friend. Wait, no, not just a best friend but part of my family. You know more than anybody how much my family means to me, and I let you be part of it. You promised me, Levi — you promised *my mom* — that you'd always be there for me. Some promise."

I felt sick to my stomach.

She wiped away a tear and continued. "I understand how important it is for you to have your guy friends, I do. But I can count on one hand the amount of times I've seen you in the past month. The past *month*, Levi. And don't forget, one of those times was so we could go shopping to get a suit for you to take that junior girl to her prom."

She was helpful, picking out the corsage I gave Jill.

"I gave up one of my closest friends because of you, Levi. Because I thought the friendship we had was worth it. But the second you get guy friends, you push me aside. Do you have any idea how worthless you've made me feel? Did you even once think about my feelings every time you canceled on me?"

Because Keith always had the worst timing, he came down the hallway right then. "Come on, California! You coming or not?" he called out.

Macallan glared at him before she turned back to me. "Please don't let me get in the way of your precious bro time." She rolled her eyes.

That's when I snapped. I no longer felt sorry for her. I was sick of the way she always made me feel like the things I wanted were stupid. That her time was more important than mine. For the way she kissed me and pretended it was nothing. That there were no consequences for her when it comes to me.

"This is all a joke for you, isn't it?" I spat at her.

Her face turned white. "I never thought —"

I cut her off. "Yep, you *never think*."

And then I walked away from her.

I had no desire to hear what she had to say anymore. I didn't like being made to feel like I was letting her down. That I was a failure somehow. That I was single-handedly responsible for her happiness. That I was the one responsible for her not being friends with Emily anymore. It was a decision *she* had made. And it wasn't my fault she wasn't with Ian anymore, either. She needed to stop putting so much on our friendship.

I was a fifteen-year-old guy. What was so wrong with wanting to hang out with my friends? My *real* friends.

I went with Keith, but it was like I wasn't there. I caught the ball because I needed to catch the ball. But that was it. My mind was back in that hallway. My mind would not move.

I wasn't proud of myself for making Macallan sad or knowing full well she was probably crying at that very second, somewhere out of my reach.

But she just got to me.

I hated that she was making me feel guilty, when she was the one who should've been —

I mean, she was the one who, like, wanted to —

I was so angry, I couldn't even think straight. I hated that I felt that way. I hated that I used to be able to tell Macallan everything, but couldn't anymore.

She drove me nuts. She had these certain ways about her that would fill me with rage when I thought about it.

The way she would tease me.

The way she would expect me to be there for her.

The way she would rest her head on my shoulder when we'd watch a movie.

The way she would taunt me by messing up my hair.

The way she kissed me and pulled away.

Really, when I thought about it, it was that moment. That kiss was when I started to feel differently about her.

But to her it was nothing.

Why did it have to be nothing?

Why couldn't it have been something?

Why did she have to pull away?

Why couldn't she —

And then it hit me.

I knew I could sometimes be slow with things, but why on earth had it taken me so long to realize what was really going on?

What I really felt. Why I was really mad. Why I was pushing Macallan away. Why being with her became more and more difficult. Why I felt nervous and angry anytime a guy mentioned her.

The second I admitted it to myself, I knew it had been true for a very, very long time.

I was in love with Macallan.

I dropped the ball and left it there on the ground. Keith asked me what was going on. I yelled something to him and the other guys about needing to talk to Macallan and ran.

I knew *love* was a strong word for someone my age. But that was what it was. That was what we had.

And I wasn't going to let it go.

We'd hit rock bottom, but this is what I found there. The truth.

I ran faster than I'd ever run before. There wouldn't have been a one-tenth difference that day. I would've blown away every last runner that time. Because at the end of this finish line wasn't a trophy — it was Macallan.

I was a little winded when I knocked on the door. I didn't care that I was sweating and probably looked a little crazy.

What I was about to *do* was crazy.

What I was about to do would change everything.

But I couldn't hold it in any longer. The truth I was concealing was driving her away.

It was time I stopped messing around and stepped up.

"Oh, hello, Levi," Mr. Dietz greeted me at the door, and he did not look very happy to see me.

"Hi, Mr. Dietz. Can I speak to Macallan, please?" I almost didn't recognize my own voice, there was so much pleading in it.

He sighed, but opened the door. "She's out back."

I went through the house and saw Adam, who looked at me stone-faced. I've never seen him look so serious. That was when I knew I was in big trouble. I went to the door to the deck, where Macallan was sitting on the steps that led to the yard. My heart almost broke when I saw there were crumpled-up tissues at her side. I slid open the glass door, and her dad stopped me from closing it.

"Levi's here," he announced. She turned around and her eyes were red. "You going to be okay, Calley?"

I'd never heard her dad call her anything but Macallan. This was worse than I'd thought.

She gave him a tiny nod.

Then I heard Adam's voice. "I'm going to be standing right here if you need anything. Anything at all." He nodded sternly at me, like he wouldn't hesitate for a second to take me down.

Adam's loyalty was a stark contrast to how I'd been behaving. I'd never been so ashamed of myself.

"Hey," I said as I gently maneuvered myself next to her on the step. "I know I've been saying this a lot lately, Macallan, but I'm sorry. I was being a grade-A jerk. I was confused about a lot of things and was trying to fit in. But I realize that none of it matters, none of it matters to me. I mean, except you."

I'd never had to declare my love to anybody before. But I was pretty confident I was doing a horrible job.

"I got so mad, because, I think, I mean, I know now that, well, I have feelings. I mean, you know, not just feelings, but I . . . Let me start over."

"You made a promise to me, Levi. You promised you'd be there for me. But you haven't been. And I never, *never* saw you as my 'whipping boy' at my 'beck and call.'"

Those words, the words I used just hours earlier, stung. I could only imagine how much they'd hurt her.

She continued while tightly holding on to a tissue. "I didn't realize what a burden it was for you to hang out with me."

"No," I said forcefully. I couldn't believe she would have ever thought that, no matter what I said. But I *had* been ignoring her. So I guess I could see why she thought that.

She disregarded my comment. "It's great that you've got your own friends. It would be selfish of me to keep you from them. That was never my intention."

"No, that's not it. I'm horrified that you would ever think that." I took her hand in mine. "I've been a complete idiot. And I know why I've been so confused. I guess I have problems expressing myself and, um . . ."

She wouldn't even look at me. I cautiously took my other hand and gently maneuvered her head so she looked at me. Her eyes were filled with tears.

"Macallan, I, I love you." It was as if those words lifted a ton of weight off my back.

"I love you, too. You're my best friend." She gave me a weak smile.

I didn't think my love and her love were the same.

"No, Macallan." I brushed her face lightly with my thumb. "That's not what I mean."

I pulled her closer to me and leaned in. We were only inches apart. My body tingled with the anticipation of another kiss. One that didn't have to end so abruptly.

Macallan's eyes widened when she realized what I was about to do. She jumped to her feet. "I'm going to Ireland," she blurted out, her voice a lot louder and higher than normal.

"You're *what*? When?"

"I'm going to Ireland to spend the summer with my mom's family. I'm leaving in a week." She said it in such a dead tone, I almost didn't believe her.

"Macallan, please." I had a feeling I was responsible for this last-minute escape route. "When did you decide this?"

"Just . . . recently." She was a horrible liar. "You know they've asked me every summer."

"So why now?"

"Why not?"

WHY NOT? WHY NOT? I wanted to scream. *BECAUSE I JUST CONFESSED MY LOVE TO YOU, THAT'S WHY NOT!*

She took a step back. "Look, Levi, I know things have been . . . different. And now you have your summer to hang out with your friends and we can pick things up again when I get back."

"Pick up what exactly?" I was testing her. Was she going to acknowledge that I wasn't telling her I loved her only as a friend?

She looked lost. "This! Our friendship." That word stung. "Clearly we need some time away from each other. You need some time with the guys, I need some time with my family. We need to figure out how to make this work. I don't want to get in your way. So I'm giving you the freedom you so desperately want."

"Macallan," I pleaded. I went to grab her hand and she backed farther away.

"It'll be fine," she tried to assure me. But I wasn't sold. "I've been thinking it was time for me to visit. Really, I'd been thinking about going this year for a while. You can ask Danielle."

Now I cursed myself for never answering my stupid phone. Maybe one of those times she was going to ask my opinion. If only I had answered.

She tried to pretend everything was normal. "It's not that big of a deal. We'll email and chat while I'm gone, and if you're lucky, I might bring you back a leprechaun."

I didn't know if I should feel relieved that she was making a joke like normal, or if I should be devastated that she certainly wasn't going to confess any un-friendlike feelings toward me.

We were at a standstill. I knew I had two options at that point. I could confess my love to her again and make her realize we could be more than friends. Or I could swallow my pride and keep whatever was left of our friendship intact.

"A leprechaun, huh? I bet it would probably fit in the overhead compartment."

I hated myself for it, but I didn't want to push her any further away.

Who knew how far she was willing to go to avoid me?

Ireland was far enough.

Just so we're remembering this correctly: When you kissed me, I went home and splashed cold water on my face. When I tried to kiss you, you ran away to Ireland for the summer.

Perhaps not the best timing on my part.

Understatement of the millennium.

CHAPTER ELEVEN

I had a lot of time to think about what I was running away from. I had the two-hour drive with Dad and Uncle Adam to O'Hare Airport. I had the connection in Boston. I had the long flight to Shannon Airport. And then the drive with Gran and Gramps to Dingle.

At one point I stopped thinking about what time it was back home. I only concentrated about what was waiting for me in Ireland.

Which wasn't much of anything.

I loved seeing my grandparents, but the town of Dingle was tiny. I'd only visited my grandparents once, years ago. Mom and I had visited two summers *before*. We went when they still lived and worked in Limerick. Then they decided to retire and move to this quiet fishing village.

Gran got a part-time job at the tourist center while Gramps worked on a book tracing the origins of famous Irish folk songs. Gran said that was his typical Irish excuse to go to pubs at night and listen to music. I always laughed when

Gran made fun of Gramps's Irish ways, because she sounded more and more like an Irish-born person with each year.

One of my favorite things about my grandparents was their story. They'd met their first week at college in Madison. Gramps said he fell in love with her when he spotted her across the quad during orientation. He was too shy to talk to her that day. He beat himself up over it all weekend. Then he walked into his first class the following Monday and saw her sitting next to the only other empty seat in class. He went right up to her and told her he thought she was the most beautiful human being on earth. And then the teacher started class. Gramps said he could hardly breathe for the rest of the class, especially when he realized he was in the wrong classroom. But instead of excusing himself, he waited until it was done. He thought Gran was taking diligent notes, but instead she was writing him a letter since she had noticed him as well. The letter was read at their wedding, after graduation.

I felt that was how people should fall in love. Instant connection.

So Gramps and Gran stayed in the States. They had my mom. But Gramps got offered a teaching job back in Ireland when I was a baby. So they went and would visit us every summer.

Now I was visiting them. They almost didn't know what to do with me.

Unfortunately, I wasn't much help.

"Can I please help you with that?" I asked Gran as she readied supper.

"You sit right there. You've had a long trip."

I sat down at the kitchen table. I should've been exhausted, but I think I was the kind of tired that made you super hyper.

"You should join me tonight at the pub to hear some real music," Gramps said, sitting down next to me.

"James Mullarkey, you're not taking our only grandchild to a pub on her first night in town."

"You're right." He rubbed his faded ginger beard. "That's more of a Wednesday night activity." He winked at me.

Gran groaned. "Macallan, honey, I have tomorrow off and thought we'd go around town. I can introduce you to some of the townsfolk. We've been telling everybody about your visit."

"She'd have a better chance meeting people of her generation at the pub."

"That's enough from you!" Gran pointed a wooden spoon at Gramps.

"Now, now." Gramps got up and went into the kitchen to wrap his arms around Gran. It was sweet how much in love they still were after all these years. "I promise to be a good influence on our dear, young, impressionable granddaughter." Gramps had his back to me so I could see him crossing his fingers behind his back.

"Shoot!" Gran pulled away. "I forgot to pick up some thyme at the store."

I stood up. "I can go get it. I'd like to go for a walk — I've been sitting for too long." I tried to do the math in my head of how many hours, maybe even days, I'd been awake.

It took me only a few minutes to get my bearings in town. There was basically the harbor front and Main Street. Plus, if I got lost, all I had to do was ask where Jim and Betty's place was. It was that small a town.

Since I had some time before dinner would be finished, I decided to go down to Dingle Harbor and watch a few boats come in. I wandered in one of the tourist shops and grabbed a few postcards. Then I made my way past the colorful buildings to the small grocery store a few blocks from my grandparents' place. I picked up the fresh thyme and waited behind an older woman who was getting in a great debate about whether or not some guy was cheating on his wife.

"I'll help you over here," I heard a voice call out. I went to the other register and handed the bunch of sprigs to a young guy with messy black hair. "Once you get me mum started, you'd be waiting all night."

"Thanks."

He smiled at me. "Ah, I didn't think you looked familiar. American?"

"Yes." I felt embarrassed that I could be figured out so easily. I'd only said one word.

"Tourist?" He helped me figure out which coins I needed to pay.

"Yes, well, no. Um, my grandparents live —"

Recognition lit his face. "Ah, you're Jim and Betty's."

"Yes."

"Is this Jim and Betty's?" The woman behind the other register came over.

"Hi, I'm Macallan." I held my hand out.

"Welcome!" The woman bypassed my hand and hugged me

against her slight frame. "We've heard so much about you. You're from America."

"Yes, outside Milwaukee, in Wisconsin. It's near Chicago."

"Pleased to meet you. I'm Sheila O'Dwyer, and this is my son, Liam."

"Hi." I gave him a shy wave, which he returned with a hearty laugh.

Sheila quickly ran off to help a new customer.

"So, Macallan from outside Milwaukee, Wisconsin," Liam said with a crooked smile.

"Sorry, I didn't know . . ." I felt so stupid. I should've just said I was from America.

"No, 'tis fine. I love the States. Madison is the capital of Wisconsin, and Milwaukee is the biggest city. I even watch your American football sometimes. The Packers, right?"

I couldn't help but instantly like him. A fellow Packers fan in Ireland?

I felt my cheeks get hot. Danielle kept teasing me I'd meet a boy named Seamus O'Leary McHunky, and here I was meeting a Liam my first day.

Liam enthusiastically continued. "I hope to study abroad there while at university. I'm thinking either Boston or New York City or California." I cringed at the mention of Levi's former home. Liam pretended to not notice. "Have you been?"

"Oh, I went to New York once when I was little. I spend a lot of time in Chicago, since it's nearby."

"Ah, yes, the Windy City!" Liam pointed his finger in the air. "I'd love to talk to you about America sometime. And I will have you know that I do love Ireland, especially our fair peninsula. I'd happily be your guide."

"That would be great."

Liam smiled at me, and I felt a flutter. "Grand."

I found myself walking back to Gran and Gramps's with an extra bounce in my step. After supper, I wrote out my postcards before bed and stared at the one for Levi for far too long. I never overthought things with him. But I had trouble figuring out what to say. Things had been tense before I left. At first I was mad at him for ignoring me. Then he came over and tried to kiss me. For a few seconds I thought it was a dare from one of the guys, but I could tell he was confused. So was I. I knew it would be best for us to have a break, but it still felt weird to not write him. I didn't want things to be strained between us. If I wanted things to return to normal, I needed to start acting like everything was fine between us. And if it wasn't, I would fake it.

Dear Levi, greetings from Dingle (insert joke here)!

I'm sure I'll have already talked to you by the time the owls have delivered this, but I wanted you to see where I'm spending the summer. Isn't it beautiful? Wow, jealousy really doesn't become you. I hope things are going well with your American football practice (yes, I've already changed so much). I must now go back to the flat and use the lift and the loo.

As they say in An Daingean, Sláinte!
Macallan

It took me nearly an hour to figure out how to sign it. *Love* would've been too charged, and anything else would've felt calculated. Which was exactly how my *cheers* in Gaelic felt.

I gave up for the evening and let sleep take over. I had the whole summer to fret about Levi, but for now I wanted to enjoy a good night's sleep before my sightseeing date with Liam.

It took me only a couple days in Dingle to wonder why I'd been resisting coming to visit the past few years. It wasn't that I didn't want to visit my grandparents, but I guess I thought it would be strange. However, it was anything but.

It was quickly becoming the best summer of my life.

I'd start every morning with a run or bike ride and witness the green sprawling landscape, the jagged mountains, and dark blue waters. I never thought my little Milwaukee suburb was a concrete jungle, but compared to this, it was Manhattan. I'd come home and make lunch for my grandparents, then either sit outside and read or go to one of the restaurants in town and help out in the kitchen. I was determined to make "proper" fish 'n' chips for everybody when I got home. Or I'd go get some Murphy's Ice Cream. Hence the need for the daily run.

Or I'd hang out with Liam.

And it didn't go without notice.

"So" — Gran linked elbows with me as we went for our daily stroll — "that Liam's a nice fella. You two seem to be getting on quite well."

"Yeah," I admitted. There wasn't really much more to say beyond that. We'd hang out and have a good time. He was a nice distraction.

But I wasn't kidding myself. Liam was cute and that accent made him even more swoon-worthy. But I also knew the last thing I needed was to complicate my life further by getting involved with another guy. I didn't even know if he liked me that way. And if he did, it was probably because I was the mysterious new girl from a faraway land.

I couldn't help but laugh.

"What's so funny?" Gran asked.

"I was thinking about how different my reception in Dingle has been to when Levi first came to school."

"How is Levi? You haven't said much about him." I studied Gran's face and found the same cheekbones and eyes as Mom's. I wondered if this was what Mom would've looked like if she'd had the opportunity to grow older. "Macallan?"

"Oh, he's fine." We walked for a few minutes in silence. I'm sure she thought I was thinking about Levi, but instead I was thinking about Mom. How much she would've loved being here with us. "Gran, do you think about Mom often?"

She stopped in her tracks, sadness overwhelming her delicate features. "Every minute of every day."

"Me too," I confessed.

"It's important to remember her. She would've been so proud of you, Calley. You look more and more like her every day." She reached up and stroked my hair. "The worst thing we could ever do is forget about her. And believe me, it gets easier every day to bring up the memories."

I nodded. It was still hard. At first I was in shock, then angry. Anytime I thought about her, I was mad. Furious that she was taken from me. So I tried desperately to get her out of my mind. But no matter how much homework and cooking I did, she was always there. And then it became comforting to me.

Because even though she wasn't physically there, she would always be with me.

"You know what I think we should do?" Gran asked.

"Go get ice cream at Murphy's?"

She laughed the same laugh as Mom. "Well, of course, but I also think that every night at dinner, we should share a favorite memory of your mother. Would you like that?"

Four years ago, I would've hated it. Four months ago, I would've felt uncomfortable about it. But now, here, I was finally ready to celebrate my mother's life with others.

"I'd like that." I paused. "And I think Mom would really like it as well."

She gave me a little squeeze. "Yes, she would."

We continued walking, both of us inside our own thoughts. Although I was pretty sure I knew what occupied our minds.

There was almost a lightness to me once we started our ritual. Every night we'd tell a story, usually a funny one. Gran and Gramps would break out their old photo albums and I'd be amazed at how similar I looked to Teen Mom.

It had taken me a long time to open up to Levi about Mom.

But now I found it easier to talk about her. I'd even mentioned her a few times to Liam.

"She sounds brilliant," Liam said as he drove us around the peninsula.

"She was." I took in the breathtaking views. It didn't matter that I'd been there for over a month; I still hadn't gotten used to the sheer magnitude of the beauty.

"By the way, you should've come last night." Liam glanced at me. "It was great crack."

I was stunned into silence.

He started laughing. "Oh, relax, Yank, it's *C-R-A-I-C*. *Craic* means good fun, conversation, atmosphere. Did ya think we were doing drugs?"

"No, of course not." Although I totally had.

"Here we are." Liam pulled off to the side of the road. We were surrounded by lush green hills. And down below, we could make out the tiny town of Dingle.

"It's gorgeous."

"You haven't seen anything yet." Liam led me to another rocky hill, which had a small waterfall flowing into it. "What do you think?"

I started to carefully climb up the rocks. "It's amazing. Thank you so much."

"Well, I plan on you giving me the ultimate American tour when I come to the States."

I turned around to say something to him when my foot missed the rock. Before I knew it, I was ankle deep in mud.

"No!" I pulled my foot out, but it was too late. My entire canvas shoe was covered.

Liam jumped up to help me back down. "Well, that won't do." He bent down and removed my shoe. I was horrified by my clumsiness. He went over to a shallow puddle of water and started cleaning off the mud. I could do nothing but stand there with my one foot off the ground, hoping I wouldn't fall over from my lack of balance.

The shoe was considerably cleaner, yet it was soaking wet. We both stared at my dripping, dirty shoe, before Liam shrugged and took both his shoes off. "You know the saying, when in Dingle . . ."

I laughed and removed my other shoe. We explored the rest of the area in bare feet. He reached out his hand to me on a particularly steep climb.

"Thanks, Levi."

Liam gave me a questioning look. "Levi?"

"Huh?"

"You said 'Thanks, Levi.' Who's Levi?"

"Oh, I did? That's odd." What *was* odd was that I hadn't yet mentioned Levi to Liam or vice versa. "Levi's a friend from home."

Liam raised his eyebrows. "A friend, huh?"

"Yes, aren't guys and girls allowed to be friends in Ireland?"

"It depends on if you want to be friends with a girl." He came over and put his hand on my waist. "Or if you want something more. So what do you want?"

I held my breath. I didn't know what he was asking exactly. Did I want something more with him or something more with Levi? I clearly didn't know the answer to either.

Part of me thought a little vacation romance might be nice,

but I still hadn't fully figured out what to do with Levi. We'd been talking more and more each week I was there. But it didn't change the reason I was currently thousands of miles away from him. From home.

"Excuse me." A recognizable accent broke me from my thoughts. We looked down to see a middle-aged American couple. "Would you take our picture?"

"Of course." I hopped down and snapped their photo, grateful for the interruption.

Liam began chatting with the couple when he found out they were from Dallas. He wanted to know about everything from cowboy boots to the Cowboys and barbecue. It really was adorable how dorky he was about all things American.

Liam excused himself from the Texans when he got a call on his phone. "Brilliant!" he exclaimed. If I had learned anything in my few weeks in Ireland, it was that everything was *brilliant*: food, music, an idea, possibly a kiss. . . . It was such a better word than *awesome* or *amazing*. I was thinking of bringing it back with me as a linguistic souvenir, but when I'd tried it out on Levi when we were video chatting, he'd laughed at me. Then he did a minute or two of re-creating everything I'd said, but in an exaggerated cockney accent. I would've been angry if it hadn't been hysterical.

"So, me mates are having a party at the beach," Liam filled me in. "Shall we?"

"Only if there'll be tons of *craic*," I fired back.

He laughed. "Totally." We headed to his car. "Not so fast, Yank."

I groaned. "Sorry!" I always went to the driver's side of the car there. I hadn't gotten used to it being on the opposite side.

We headed to Clogher Strand, one of my favorite places to sit and relax. It wasn't a beach for swimming because of the currents, but it had a gorgeous view of the Blasket Islands. I had met only a couple of Liam's friends at that point, Conor and Michael, who referred to me simply as "the American." I wasn't sure if they actually knew my name. Although I was more than aware that they were familiar with my Scottish namesake.

"Liam!" Conor cried out while we made our way to the blankets they'd lined up on the sand. "And you brought the American."

Conor handed Liam a bottle, then turned to me. "Can we tempt you?"

"I'm good." *And only fifteen*, I thought.

"You Americans are so uptight about alcohol." Conor laughed and went to sit with the other group.

"Are you okay?" Liam asked.

"Yeah." Although I didn't think I was.

I saw Liam grimace slightly at someone who was behind me.

"Is everything all right?" I went to turn around, but he stopped me.

"Yeah, well, no . . . 'Tis me ex, Siobhan." He took a quick swig of his bottle.

I'd heard him mention Siobhan a few times. "Do you want to talk about it?"

He shrugged. "Not much to say. We dated for a year, she fancied another fella, and we broke up. 'Tis fine, except things are awkward. Mostly for me. It's hard to be reminded that you weren't good enough for someone, ya know?"

"I understand," I said. "That's sort of how I feel about Levi."

"I thought you said you were just friends."

"We were. *Are.* But then he wanted more. I don't know."

Liam looked around the beach. "I'm fine leaving if you want to go back to town. Let me go say bye to Conor and Michael."

He walked off while I stood there awkwardly. Then I heard a familiar name.

"Sorry," I interrupted a group that was near me. "Were you talking about *Buggy and Floyd*? I love that show."

The guy who was talking exchanged a look with a girl with dark hair. "Um, yeah. I was saying that they're apparently doing a Christmas special."

"Really?" I asked excitedly. "They haven't had any new episodes in over five years."

The girl scowled at me. "That show is so lame. I'm only interested in it because the guy who played the younger brother is hot now."

I smiled at her as a memory surfaced. "I know who you're talking about. He's hilarious! Remember the episode where Floyd got locked up in the school gym with him?" I started laughing at the memory of Levi repeatedly imitating Buggy looking into the gym window and saying, "Blimey if I knew you'd be here; you're not really the fit type."

"Whatever." The black-haired girl went back to ignoring me.

Right then I recognized the feeling that was steadily growing inside me. I absolutely loved Dingle. I loved being with my grandparents. And everybody (present company excluded) had been so warm and welcoming. But this wasn't my home. These people weren't my friends.

Truth be told, what was really bothering me was Levi. I missed him. I'd started missing him when I was still home, while we were still in school together. I wanted him to be next to me. He would've loved Dingle, this beach, this beautiful view.

But he wasn't here.

Liam approached me with a resigned smile. "Ready to go home?"

Yes, yes, I was.

Liam opened up about his relationship with Siobhan on the drive back to my grandparents'. They'd known each other since childhood and had the tight-knit group of friends you'd expect in such a tiny village. Then they decided to date. Now they didn't even talk anymore. Liam couldn't even be on the same beach as her.

It gave me a lot to think about. And all those thoughts revolved around Levi. I had to talk to him. To make sure that we were still friends. That we'd still be able to be in the same room together when I got home.

Fortunately, my grandparents were out, so I was able to go right to my room and dial Levi on my laptop the second I was dropped off. I did the math and knew he would, hopefully, be getting home from morning practice. My leg was shaking by the third ring.

All I kept thinking to myself was *Please be home, Levi. Please be home.*

The screen lit up and I saw Levi's naked chest in front of me.

"Um, hello?" I asked, feeling my cheeks get hot at the sight of Levi's body.

"Hey!" He adjusted the towel around his waist. "Sorry, just got out of the shower." He walked out of view for a few seconds and returned with a T-shirt on. His hair was wet and sticking up in different directions.

"Hey, you!" I was smiling ear to ear.

"Well, hello to you!"

"*Buggy and Floyd* are doing a Christmas special!" I blurted.

His eyes lit up. "Are you serious? That is *bloody brilliant*." He winked at me.

"Ha. Ha." I stuck my tongue out at him.

"I see being abroad has really helped with your maturity."

"Totally."

He opened his mouth to say something, but then he tilted his head as if he was studying me. "Are you okay?"

It was the same question Liam had asked me not thirty minutes before. I gave him the same answer. "Yeah."

But here was the difference between Liam and Levi: Levi knew when I was full of it.

"What's wrong?" The genuine caring on his face almost made me cry.

"Just a little homesick," I admitted.

I was surprised by Levi's reaction. He smiled.

"Oh, I'm sorry," I said. "Are you enjoying my misery?"

He shook his head. "No, it's . . . you always seem so happy whenever we talk, and I want you to be happy, but I also want you to get home already. I miss having someone to laugh at my lame jokes. And, well, I miss you."

"I miss you, too."

There was a silence between us. Not because we were uncomfortable but because we didn't really need to say anything else. We both felt the same thing.

I finally spoke. "But, hey, I'm sure the next three weeks will fly by."

"Actually, it's sixteen days," he corrected me.

"Oh, so you're counting?" I teased.

"Duh. It's on my calendar. *Macallan returns and life officially doesn't suck anymore.*"

"So are you saying your life would suck without me? I'm assuming you're quoting Kelly Clarkson because you miss having such a strong, independent girl like myself around."

"Ha! Nicely played. But of course." He paused. *"Here's the thing, we started out friends. . . ."*

I laughed. "Wait, are you now insinuating that since I've been gone, you can breathe for the first time?"

"Wait, no!"

I shook my head. "You really are becoming unraveled without me."

He had that familiar crooked smile on his face. "I know. See, you go away and I can't think straight. It's amazing I can even get up in the morning."

"Oh, how I miss your dramatics."

"Nobody else appreciates them like you do."

"I know."

"So let me make sure I get this," Liam said to me as we waited in line at Murphy's to get some ice cream a couple nights later. "Your best friend is a guy. He likes you as more than just a friend. And your response was to run away to Ireland?"

"Well, when you put it that way . . ." I tried to joke, but I started to feel a little silly. "There was a lot more going on."

"Ah, right." He nodded. "He started to hang out with his guy friends."

"And was ignoring me," I reminded him.

I'd decided to open up to Liam about Levi. I figured nothing was going to happen between us; we both had too much baggage. So maybe it would be helpful to get an outside opinion on the subject. But unfortunately, I had a feeling he was going to take Levi's side.

I guess bros gotta stick with bros.

We placed our orders. Liam always got Guinness and brown bread, which didn't taste as bad as one would think. I ordered my favorite combination: sea salt and honeycomb.

After we grabbed our cones, I decided to make one last plea for my case. "And remember, I basically don't see him for months, then we get into a fight and *then* he comes over and tells me he loves me. It was so out of the blue."

Liam took a lick of his cone. "Was it really?"

My response was to be really into eating my ice cream. Which I was, but I also didn't have a proper response.

"But you only think of him as a friend," Liam stated, and I could tell that he didn't believe me. "You're not attracted to him at all?"

"No. I mean yes. I mean, he's Levi."

"'He's Levi'? Is that some sort of Yank expression I'm not aware of?" he teased. "So he's your best friend. He's a

Levi, whatever that means. I don't really see what the problem is."

"It's difficult." I began to walk faster to the harbor.

"Yes, you keep reminding me of that. But here's the thing. It doesn't sound that difficult. You're only making it difficult. It sounds like there's a lot between you. Don't be afraid to make it even more."

I smiled tightly, not sure if I should believe him or not. So I played it lightly. "Since when did you become some sort of relationship expert?"

He looked at me amusedly. "'Tis common sense, really."

I faced the harbor, which was lined up with buses bursting with tourists. "So I better go see this dolphin."

Ever since I'd arrived in Dingle, everybody had been asking me if I'd seen Fungie, the town dolphin. There was a statue of him right next to the information center where Gran worked. I'd gotten my picture taken with the statue my first week there but hadn't seen Fungie yet.

"It is rather shocking that you've been here for six weeks and haven't gone." Liam took out his phone and gestured at me to pose for yet another photo by the statue. "Have some pride in Dingle, will ya?"

I sulked next to the statue. "It feels a bit touristy."

"Right. Because you're *not* a tourist." He snapped the photo. "We've got to make sure to get everything in over the next few days. Because you'll be home soon. So there's lots to do. Including a decision that needs to be made."

He didn't have to remind me.

<hr>

The next two weeks flew by. Gran and Gramps did everything to make sure I got to see as much as I could before I left. I was almost too tired for my farewell party, but if there was one thing I'd learned during my two months in Ireland, it was that the Irish knew how to throw a good party.

My grandparents' backyard was transformed into an impromptu music session. We hung up fairy lights around the trees to make it even more magical. Gran and Gramps's friends, who had become like an extended family to me, started trickling into the backyard. Some of Gramps's musician friends brought their instruments, and music soon started to fill the cool evening.

Liam arrived with his mom. "Hey, I brought you something to remember me by," he said. He handed me a CD; the cover was the photo of me with the Fungie statue. I opened up the case and saw a listing of Irish bands he'd introduced me to during my visit. "While I love all things American, we Irish have superior music. Not like you have any Yank bands on your iTunes, you Anglophile. So it's time you heard some proper, non-U2 Irish bands."

"Thanks!" I gave him a hug, grateful to have had him around during my visit.

Gramps asked everybody to quiet down. "I want to thank you all for coming here to bid our favorite granddaughter good-bye."

"Your *only* granddaughter," I clarified.

There was laughter from the guests.

"But I think it would only be appropriate to send Macallan off with a parting glass."

There were nods from their friends, who lifted up a glass. I joined them in the toast, but was unfamiliar with the song they started to play.

Gramps looked at me fondly and began to sing,

Of all the money that e'er I had,
I spent it in good company.
And all the harm that e'er I've done
Alas, it was to none but me.
And for all I've done for want of wit,
To mem'ry now I can't recall.

Everybody joined in at this part:

So fill to me the parting glass.
Good night and joy be with you all.

Gran then joined Gramps as he wrapped his arm around her. She sang in a clear beautiful voice:

To all the comrades that e'er I had,
They're sorry for my going away.

She smiled warmly at me.

And all the sweethearts that e'er I had,
They'd wish me one more day to stay.
But since it falls unto my lot,
That I should rise and you should not,

I'll gently rise and softly call.
Good night and joy be with you all.

I felt tears rolling down my face. I should've been sad about leaving my grandparents and this wonderful place, but the tears weren't for them.

And Liam knew it. "I'll make it simple for you," he said, leaning in. "If you want to be with him, be with him."

My throat felt tight. "I can't."

He shook his head. Liam often teased me about making things difficult — *typical American*, he'd fondly call me. "I'd ask why, but you and I both know there isn't any excuse good enough. Stop making excuses and be with him."

I knew he was right. And it terrified me.

"Do you want to be with him?"

I didn't think. I answered what I knew was the truth. "Yes."

"Then be with him." He got up and joined the group at the front singing.

Good night and joy be with you all.

I was surprised they didn't hold me at customs since I was so shaky and nervous. As soon as I got my proper entrance stamp and baggage, I bounded for the greeting area. I ran out and didn't have to wait more than two seconds before I heard Dad, Uncle Adam, and Levi calling out for me. I turned and saw Levi holding a huge sign: BLIMEY IF WE KNOW WHERE MACALLAN IS!

I laughed and ran up to them. There was a flurry of hugs and exchanges of "I missed you" and "You look great!" Dad and Adam took my luggage and went to get the car while Levi waited with me outside.

"I'm so glad you're home," he said. He wrapped his arm around me and I fell into him. We both stayed there for a while. It felt right. It had always felt right. But I'd kept telling myself that it would ruin our friendship. Never had I thought about how it could make things even better between us. I knew the average high school couple rarely made it work long-term, but there was nothing average about Levi and me.

I heard his phone go off, and he silenced it. I closed my eyes again, grateful to be back with him. Back home. Happy that the awkwardness we'd had when I left had been erased. I reached for his hand and entwined his fingers with mine. I was debating telling him everything right there and then, but the last thing I wanted was for my dad and uncle to drive up during that conversation, especially if it ended in a kiss. I was pretty sure my dad would be making up new rules about when and where we could be together if he saw that.

Levi's phone went off again. He reached to silence it again, and I noticed an unfamiliar name on the screen.

"Who's Stacey?" I asked before I had a chance to stop myself.

Levi pulled away from me. "Oh, yeah, that." He shuffled uncomfortably. "I wanted to wait for you to be settled in before I told you that you and Stacey would not be allowed to be at parties together." He laughed lightly.

Why would this girl and I not be allowed to go to . . .

No.

It hit me like a wall of bricks.

"You have a girlfriend."

"Well, we've been hanging out — I'm not sure I'd say *girl-friend* yet. But she's cool. Stacey Hobbs — she's our year and on the cheerleading squad."

"Oh." I knew who he was talking about, but I was trying to figure out how this had happened and why Levi had conveniently neglected to mention anything to me about it. I found myself stepping away from him a bit, needing some distance to try to make sense of it all.

"But enough about me. Tonight is all about you." Levi stepped forward. "I should warn you that Mom's obsessed with making shepherd's pie for you tonight to ease you back into the Midwest. And you know how paranoid she gets cooking for you, so throw in some *brilliant*s and all will be good."

I gave him a weak smile.

"Come here. I missed you so much." He put his arms around me again. "I don't think I'm going to be able to let go. Having your best friend leave you for the summer blows." He kissed me on the forehead. "But I promise to stop being jealous and want to hear every detail of your trip. I want to be inundated with photos and stories that will make me green with envy. I mean it. You have to tell me *everything*."

But I really couldn't tell him *everything*, since there was one thing I had to keep to myself.

Awk-ward!

Dude, do you realize if you'd said something right then, everything would've been different?

Like you would no longer call me dude?

Whatever, *dude*. But don't pretend that I'm the one into drama when you yourself led us into more drama.

You got me there.

So you're admitting that I'm totally right?

No. Because you have to admit life is more interesting with a little drama.

Are you serious? Life is more of a pain in the rear with drama.

Oh, wait, you're totally right on that one. My bad.

CHAPTER TWELVE

I was so stoked to have Macallan back. Summer wasn't the same without her around. It wasn't until she was truly gone, thousands of miles away, that I realized how much time we spent together each summer. And yeah, even though I had my guys, it was different. It didn't feel the same. Nothing was the same without her.

At first I was mad at her for going away, but then I got it. We probably needed a break to reassess things.

I truly loved Macallan, I did. But I realized that she didn't feel the same, so if the only way I could have her in my life was as a friend, that's what we'd be.

I admit, she looked so cute when she got out of customs at the airport. She had that sleepy look she got when she was either super tired or under a lot of pressure. She was pretty quiet on the drive home and at dinner that evening. But I felt a lot better just having her near me.

I probably should've told her about Stacey while she was in Ireland, but it never had felt like the right time. Stacey was great and really cool, but truthfully I thought I should have a girlfriend by the time Macallan got back solely to avoid any more awkwardness. I didn't want her to feel uncomfortable or to think I was still pining over her. I had to put that aside if I wanted things to go back to normal.

I wish I could say that things went quickly back to how they'd been before all our problems. But Macallan started acting almost uncomfortable around me. At first I brushed it off as jet lag, I mean, she nearly cut off her finger one day in the kitchen when I asked her advice about Stacey, and Macallan was always very careful when she was cooking. So that I got. But after a week of her dropping things around me whenever I got too close to her, of her avoiding my eyes, I realized that my confession to her might've done some significant damage that would take a lot longer to repair. I was willing to give her the space, whatever she needed to feel comfortable around me again.

It was two weeks before school was starting and Macallan was busy in the kitchen with my mom. She had come over to hang out with me, but the second my mom showed up with a bag of groceries, Macallan jumped up to help her, and I hadn't seen her since.

It seemed like every time we were supposed to hang, she'd find something else to do. Someone else to be around.

I guess this was how she felt the second half of sophomore year: discarded.

If I could have taken back that confession to her, I would have. Keeping it bottled up inside probably would've destroyed me, but better my sanity than my relationship with her.

After nearly a half hour of being ignored, I decided to go into the kitchen.

Macallan was sitting at the kitchen table, not helping, not doing anything, just chatting with Mom.

"Oh, sweetie," Mom said to me, like she'd forgotten I was home. "Macallan gave me a new barbecue recipe that I'm going to try out tonight. You have to join us, Macallan. I feel like I haven't seen you that much since you got home. Plus, I need you as my expert taste tester."

Macallan beamed at Mom. "That sounds great."

"Fantastic." Mom looked over at me. "Stacey likes brats, right?"

"Yep," I replied.

Macallan hit her head. "Oh my goodness, today's Wednesday, right? I thought it was Tuesday. I have something tonight."

"Aww, that's too bad." Mom looked genuinely sad. "Levi, how did your driving class go today?"

"Good, I've almost mastered parallel parking. I was thinking that I really want to take my driver's license test on my actual birthday." My sixteenth birthday was in a few weeks and I had my fingers crossed for a car.

"Sure." Mom paused. "Although you're going to have your first football game of the season the next night, so I don't want you to overbook yourself. School comes first — you know that."

"But I figured that if I got my license, then I could drive us all into Milwaukee for a birthday dinner or something."

"Hmm, again, I don't want you overdoing it. We should think about doing something low-key for your birthday. Sixteen is a big one, but I don't think we should get crazy. You can go out with your friends after the game." Her phone rang and she picked it up and went into the other room.

That was so not like my mom. She'd completely brushed my birthday aside. Mom always freaked out over my birthday. Extravagant, overplanned parties. The benefits of being an only child, I guess.

I turned toward Macallan. "Wasn't she being weird?"

She looked confused. "What?"

"My mom. Just now. She was so weird about my birthday, don't you think?"

"Huh?" Macallan looked at me like I was speaking a foreign language.

"Don't you remember how she usually is with my birthday? She always makes a big deal out of it."

Macallan's eyes got wide. "You're right — she's a monster!"

Maybe I was reading too much into it. "So is she planning something?"

"Not that I know of. Honestly."

I studied her for a second and could see she was being truthful.

"Maybe she thinks we're growing up and don't need to have a big party with clowns and balloon animals," she offered.

"But I really wanted a balloon animal in the shape of a horsey." I pretended to pout. "You're probably right, although I usually have to calm her down over my birthday, and now it's almost like she doesn't care."

Macallan dismissed me. "Wow. You're being so dramatic. Your mom is the most loving mother ever. So just chill. I think all that practice in the sun has gotten to you."

I was used to being in the sun, but being outside in the sun wearing a football uniform wasn't exactly easy on my body.

"Yeah, I guess you've got a point. Well, anyway, what do you have going on tonight?"

"Huh?"

"Tonight?" I said. She looked at me blankly. "You have some plans, so you can't stay for dinner." I decided to poke her playfully at her side, but she jumped. I wasn't used to her being this nervous around me. Something had to be going on.

Her eyes lit up. "Yes. Of course. It's a . . . a family thing I have with Uncle Adam."

"Is everything okay?"

"Uh, yeah, it's really not a big deal. I promised I'd go see a movie with him tonight." She wouldn't even look me in the eye.

"Oh, yeah, what movie?"

"Movie? Um, I forgot which one he wanted to see."

Okay, it didn't take a genius to figure out that something was going on with Macallan. She clearly had plans tonight that she didn't want me to know about. I wondered if she was already dating someone. She hadn't even been back that long. But what else could it have been? She was disappearing and making excuses to not hang out as much. She hadn't even met Stacey. I knew that she knew who she was from school, but this was different.

Whatever it was, she didn't want me to know, and I had to respect her privacy. The last thing I wanted to do was make it worse.

I used to complain about the cold weather in Wisconsin when I first moved here. But little did I realize that the August heat waves would become the bane of my existence.

Keith walked out of practice with me. "This has never happened before, California."

"You've never had a practice canceled?"

He shook his head. "Nah, this heat wave is brutal."

We walked up to his truck and he unlocked the door. "Thanks for the ride, man."

"No problem." He smirked at me. "I'm sorry I didn't bring a car seat for you."

Ugh. I couldn't wait to get my driver's license. I hated having to rely on my parents or friends to get me around, especially to practice.

"Listen, if practice doesn't work out tomorrow, you should come over and run a few plays with me. My backyard gets pretty shady in the afternoon."

"Sounds good." I paused for a second. I know guys are supposed to be chill, but I really appreciated everything Keith had done to help me with the team. "And thanks, man, for everything. I don't think I would've made varsity without you."

"Yeah, well, you're fast. We need a fast guy. But don't start writing me love letters yet." He laughed. "You've still got to get in the game and catch the ball."

"Got it. Get in the game, catch the ball, *then* write you love letters."

He pulled up outside my house. "Yeah, but I wouldn't want Macallan to get jealous. She's a tough one. If only chicks could play football."

I hopped out of the car and noticed Mr. Dietz's car parked out front. I rushed inside, calling out, "Is everything okay with Macallan?"

I stopped suddenly when I saw Mom and Mr. Dietz leaning closely together at the kitchen table. They were looking at a piece of paper.

"Oh." Mom jumped up. "What are you doing home so early?"

I looked between them. Something was off.

"Is Macallan okay?"

Mom shot Mr. Dietz a nervous glance. He stood up. "Yes, yes, she's fine. I was just in the neighborhood. . . ." He tried to grab the paper off the table nonchalantly, but it was so obvious what he was doing.

"What's that?" I motioned at the paper in his hand.

"Oh, well . . ." They exchanged another nervous look. "I was asking your mother for her opinion on some cooking stuff I was going to get Macallan for her birthday."

For some reason, I didn't buy it. "Really? Can I see it?"

"Mr. Dietz was on his way out," Mom said right as the coffeemaker went off. Mom never made coffee only for herself. She did it when we had company.

"Yes." He excused himself. "I was taking a quick break from work. You know, Levi, I was hoping to surprise Macallan with this, so if you could not tell her I was here."

I didn't like deceiving Macallan, not when our relationship was in such a fragile place. But between Macallan's behavior and our parents' secretive meeting, I couldn't help but think there was something going on that I wasn't being told.

It was all very mysterious. And I wasn't in the mood for mysterious.

In the next week, Mom and Mr. Dietz seemed to be talking on the phone a lot. Not that Mom told me it was Mr. Dietz. I had to sneak a look at her phone.

I figured Macallan might know what was going on. I headed over there the Saturday before school started. Normally, I'd just walk in, but since Macallan had been so uneasy around me lately, I knocked on the door.

"Oh, hey." I could instantly tell that Macallan didn't want to see me. She definitely knew what was going on. And I wasn't going to leave until she came clean.

We walked into the kitchen, where she had all this dough and flour on the counter.

"I'm making pasta," she said as she began working with the dough.

This was usually the part where she would invite me to stay for dinner. She always did that. But I hadn't gotten one invitation since she got back. The only time we sat down for a meal was her first night home and during our Sunday night family dinner. The thought of having to sit around their dinner table the following evening made me uneasy. There were too many unanswered questions.

I decided to not dance around the subject. "Are you keeping something from me?"

Macallan stopped cold. *I knew it.*

"What are you talking about?" She threw some flour on the dough and turned around so I couldn't see her face.

"I think there's something going on with you. You're doing that thing you do."

She tried to play it off lightly. "Cook? Yep, this is what I do now, Levi. Call in the detectives!" She laughed, but it was self-conscious, almost calculated laughter. She wanted me to brush it all off and move on.

Unfortunately for her, I wasn't going to do that.

Enough was enough.

"Come on, Macallan. I'm not an idiot. You've been distant. Our parents are talking to each other all the time. What would they have to talk about if it wasn't one of us?"

"I don't know. They're friends — aren't friends allowed to talk? Stop making it some conspiracy theory. Friends talk."

"Yes, friends talk. But that's not what you and I have been doing."

She ignored me and continued to roll out the dough. "Can you stop for a second, sit down, and talk to me? Please?" I moved a chair for her to sit down next to me.

She hesitated. She never used to be so guarded around me.

Macallan sat down with a towel in her hands. She methodically wiped the flour off her hands, still refusing eye contact.

"Macallan, can you please tell me what's going on? You've been acting different since you've gotten back, like I make you uncomfortable now."

She finally looked at me, and she looked scared. "It's only . . . I had a lot of time to think in Ireland. And things *have* been different since I've been back. I *have* been different. It's just that, I guess, it's . . ." She looked down. "Levi, I think our friendship has been through a lot lately, so I don't want to add any more tension, seriously. Can we not do this right now? Please."

I wanted to give her some space, but wasn't eight weeks in another country enough? Frustration started pouring over me. I'd always been truthful to Macallan, but I couldn't help but feel that she was lying to me. Again.

I'd been so concerned about Macallan and her feelings, but what about mine? It had hurt me when she went away. I had tried to give her everything I thought she wanted — my time, my attention — and it still hadn't been enough.

But this time it wasn't on me. *She* was the one who left. *She* was the one who wasn't around. *She* was the one who was canceling on me.

I had been there the entire time waiting for her to come back. But I still felt like she was gone.

And I was tired of waiting.

"You abandoned me." The words flew out so fast I didn't have a chance to catch them. "I confessed my feelings for you and you just walked out and abandoned me. Do you have any idea how much that hurt me? But I gave you your space and didn't say anything because I hoped once you got back, everything would be okay between us. But they're not. I don't know what else to do because *I'm* not the one acting weird."

"Oh, really?" Her voice rose sharply. "You're turning this on me? Yes, you confessed your feelings to me. You left this huge door open. Then I come home to find it slammed in my face."

"A *door*? What door did I slam in your face? I couldn't wait for you to get home!"

Instead of yelling back at me, her voice wavered. "The entire time I was in Ireland, I thought of you. You certainly gave me a lot to think about. And I did, Levi. A lot. I wanted to make this work between us. So much. I got off the plane thinking we'd have this happy ending. And then I had the rug pulled from under me. I think all the time about when the plane was landing in Chicago. How different things are now compared to what I thought they'd be. How foolish I'd been. So yes, Levi, I'm not there for you as much, but you're not here, either."

"Are you kidding me? I've *been here* the entire time, Macallan. *You* were the one who left. Left *me*. And *you're* the one who's been ignoring me. I waited months for you to return, and you're here, but you're not *really* here. So just tell me what you want from me because I'm tired of guessing and tired of feeling like I can never satisfy you. So please, enlighten me."

She opened her mouth, then closed it. Her gaze was transfixed on the floor. She refused to even look at me.

I wanted her to stand up and fight. To fight for this relationship, but I already knew she was giving up on me. And at the moment, I didn't care. Why was it solely up to me to fix things between us? Especially when I had no clue what more I could've done. But nothing I did ever seemed to be good enough for her. She always expected so much from me. And that was the heart of the problem. Macallan didn't want to share me with others.

I got up and started walking toward the door. Had she said something, I would've turned around. But she didn't.

As soon as the door was closed, the fight left me. I was exhausted by the constant questioning. All the drama.

I began walking home. Putting distance between me and my former best friend.

If this was how it was going to be, it was better to know than to pretend. I felt a newfound freedom with every step.

Maybe Macallan going to Ireland was the best thing that could have happened to me. It proved that I didn't need her to be around to be happy. Sure, I had missed her. But it was more the memory of her. How things used to be. She had changed, and so had I. It seemed we both were hanging on to someone who no longer existed.

I decided right there that all I wanted was a drama-free junior year.

If that meant it was without Macallan, so be it. I was done with her games.

We both went through the motions on Sunday nights. Fortunately, I only had to put up the act for the first two weeks of school before I started making excuses to get out of the dinners.

It didn't matter. I had an awesome birthday. The guys came over after the game. Stacey brought some of her friends. Of course, Mom invited Macallan, but, thankfully, she couldn't come. She didn't even give me anything. Her birthday was in a couple of weeks and I planned on returning the favor.

If only our family could've figured it out and stop forcing us together. Fortunately, I was always free on Saturday nights, so it could be just me and my girl. My *real* girl.

Stacey had been great about the whole Macallan thing — which meant she never really brought it up. She let us be us, which had nothing to do with that. I appreciated it.

That Saturday when she pulled up in her car, she seemed extra excited to see me.

"Hey, handsome." She bent over and gave me a kiss, her high ponytail brushing against my cheek. "I thought we'd try someplace different for dinner tonight. You in?"

"Sure." I shrugged. I wasn't in a great mood. The previous night had been our third game of the season and I still hadn't gotten any playing time. I could run fast, was getting better with catching, but Coach wasn't putting me in. I couldn't show him my frustration, so it bounced onto the other people in my life.

"Where we going?" I asked when Stacey pulled into a hotel parking lot.

"I heard the restaurant here is really good." She laughed nervously.

I got out of the car. Stacey looked at her phone. "Can you hold on? I have to make a quick call."

"Sure." A hotel seemed like a strange place for dinner. But whatever. Stacey usually knew what she was doing.

But then things got weirder.

"Levi?" I turned around and saw Macallan with Danielle. "What are you doing here?"

"What am *I* doing here? What are *you* doing here?"

Danielle looked at each of us and stepped in the middle. "So crazy, right? I guess this is the new place to be." She laughed as Stacey came over.

"Hey, guys," Stacey said warmly to Macallan. "So insane that you're here." She exchanged a look with Danielle. "Um, I guess we should go in." She started walking faster, with Danielle keeping step and saying she liked Stacey's shoes.

This left me next to Macallan.

"Are you following me?" I asked her.

She groaned. "Yeah, whatever."

"It's just a little odd that you're here. I never even knew this place had a restaurant."

"It wasn't my idea — it was Danielle's," she said coldly.

"How convenient for you."

Danielle and Stacey led us inside and stopped in front of these giant double doors.

I was so annoyed at this. That I had to be stuck eating in the same vicinity as Macallan. And I highly doubted this was a mere coincidence. She clearly couldn't handle not being around me anymore.

Macallan stopped and looked right at me as if she could read my mind. "Get over yourself, Levi." She stepped in front of me.

"After you!" Stacey said as she and Danielle opened up the double doors.

I put a scowl on my face to let them know how much I didn't appreciate this situation as I began to walk into the room.

"SURPRISE!!!" A loud shout echoed in the large ballroom. It took me a second to figure out what was going on as I saw the faces of friends and family greeting me. Then I saw a HAPPY SWEET SIXTEEN BIRTHDAY, MACALLAN AND LEVI! sign.

The secret meetings between our parents had been for a birthday party.

I turned to look at Macallan, who looked as shocked as I felt. So she hadn't been lying to me about not knowing what was going on. But she was lying about something else.

Mom came up laughing. "Did we pull it off? Were you surprised?"

I don't think I'd ever been so shocked in my life.

Talk about being oblivious.

I know, they got us so good.

I was referring to our parents. How could they not have
figured out we weren't even talking?

Yeah, we weren't speaking and they threw us a joint surprise
party.

I'm more shocked that Danielle didn't say something to my
dad. She doesn't hold things in.

Like you do?

Oh, yes, I was the one who was being irrational.

Man, I was being such an idiot.

I'm sorry, I don't believe I heard you. Could you repeat
that?

Yes, I was being an idiot, a total idiot. Even I wouldn't have wanted to
hang out with me.

And people think girls get emotional.

Again, I was really confused after *you abandoned me.*

And you wondered why I had to leave the country?

CHAPTER THIRTEEN

I was shocked at first by the unexpected group of people cheering "SURPRISE!" And the evening got even more surreal from there.

Dad came over and gave me a big hug, followed by Uncle Adam.

Dad beamed. "Here I thought you were too smart for your old pops to get you."

I looked around and saw about fifty people, from all over my life. There were mostly people from school rounded out by some family members and a few of my cooking class friends.

It wasn't hard to pick out who was for Levi and who was for me. It was like this one wedding I went to the summer *before*. Mom's friend from college was marrying a guy Mom didn't approve of. Everybody on Suzanne's side was dressed in suits or dresses. The groom's side was completely different. I heard Mom "tsk-tsk" a few times as people walked in dressed in khakis and jeans. Someone even had jorts on.

"Who wears jeans to a wedding?" Mom had asked under her breath.

I'd shrugged. I was only ten at the time, so I didn't have that great an answer.

Six years later, I still didn't have the answer for a lot of things.

Levi went over to the jock contingent. It was then I noticed Emily was there. I was pretty sure Levi's mom wouldn't have invited her. I scanned back in my head to see if I'd ever officially told my dad that we weren't really friends anymore. She hadn't been to our house in years.

Emily gave me a little wave and approached cautiously. "Happy birthday, Macallan."

"Thanks," I said as we embraced uncomfortably.

"Great party!" she said as she scanned the room.

"Yeah." It *was* a great party.

"Anyway, I know it's been a while, but it's a big day, so I got you a little something." Emily handed me a small wrapped box.

"Oh, you shouldn't have," I protested. She shrugged in response. I didn't know if I was supposed to wait to open presents, but since I hadn't even known this party was happening, I figured I could be excused for not following protocol.

I slowly unwrapped the box to find a silver necklace with a delicate flower pendant.

"It'll go with pretty much anything," Emily offered.

"Thanks so much." Emily knew I was awful at accessorizing. It was a gene that wasn't passed on to me. I unlatched the necklace and put it around my neck.

"Here, let me help." I held up my hair as Emily latched the

necklace. It fell right in the middle of the scoop neck shirt that I was wearing. "Perfect!" she declared.

I gave Emily a grateful smile. She was looking out for my girly well-being even though we were no longer close.

We looked at each other, neither of us really knowing what to do now. It was so odd to be standing across from someone who had been my best friend for nearly a decade and yet have nothing to talk about. I couldn't help but wonder if that was what was going to happen to me and Levi. We already didn't speak to each other.

I looked across and saw him laughing away with his friends. My anger at Levi wasn't that he had friends. It was that he'd filled my head with thoughts of love, then took it away from me. I tried to guard myself from getting hurt — it was an automatic reflex. But I'd let Levi in as a friend, then as a best friend. By the time I'd landed in Chicago, I'd been ready to open my heart fully to him. To love him the way I thought he loved me.

But then he'd taken it away. It was torture to be around him those first few days back.

My attention was brought back to the party as our parents were asking for everybody's attention at the front of the room. Dread filled me, because I knew something embarrassing would probably come next.

"Okay, everybody!" Dad was clinking a glass with a fork. A sharp whistle came from Uncle Adam and the place quieted down. "Thanks so much for coming tonight. And for keeping our little secret." There was some laughter in the audience. "Can the birthday girl and boy come on up here?"

Levi and I came from opposite ends of the room and were greeted by polite applause and some catcalling from the jock group.

Mrs. Rodgers looked so happy. "I have to say that I was convinced Levi was onto me, he was being really nosy and asking so many questions."

"Which should always be a cause for concern," Dr. Rodgers interjected as he put his arm around Levi's shoulder. Seeing Levi and his dad standing next to each other made me realize how much they looked alike, except for his dad's dark hair.

Levi's posture was stiff and he didn't look that amused. But then a slow smile started to spread on his face as his dad began to jostle him.

Mrs. Rodgers got back control of the room. "Bruce and I can't begin to express how much Macallan has meant to us, as well as Bill and Adam. They were so welcoming to us West Coasters and really brought us into their family." She came over and grabbed my hand. "I am so grateful that Levi has such a generous, caring best friend."

I glanced over at Levi, but his eyes were aimed at the floor. Maybe *this* was what we really needed to get everything back to how it used to be between us. Everything she was saying was true (especially about me being generous and caring; she missed humble).

I had been distant when I got back, mostly to try to adjust to the new reality that was waiting for me. Then Levi threw those hurtful words and accusations at me that day in my kitchen. I was convinced he was going to come back and apologize. But he left.

I wanted my old Levi back.

Even if it was only as friends.

The way he lashed out at me made me realize how delicate our relationship was. But he was too important to me, such a huge part of my life, I'd take him any way I could. Sure, there would always be something unspoken between us. An attraction we wouldn't act on. But would a high school romance really be worth sacrificing our friendship?

No. We were better off friends.

I kept waiting all night. Through the speeches and roasting, the singing and cake, through the dancing and presents. I was poised expectantly for Levi to come over to me and make everything right.

But I was waiting for an apology that would never come.

I don't know what compelled me to go to the last football game of the season. Uncle Adam was more than happy to join me in the bleachers. He went to every high school game, proudly wearing his orange and blue. My excuse that evening was that I was going to root for Danielle and the marching band. I even waved a few times at Emily down on the field as she cheered.

That was my excuse. Truthfully, I wanted to be there in case Levi finally got a chance to play. It wasn't that he was bad; it was only that the wide receivers on the team who got playing time were all seniors and very, very good.

I didn't know how much longer my loyalty to Levi would last. We had hardly spoken since the party. We'd pass each other in the hallways and he'd do that chin thing that lets the person know you're acknowledging her, but not so much as to grant her the pleasure of uttering a proper hello. I tried to not let it get to me, but I got more hurt with each passing day. I sometimes thought it would be best to let it go and move on. I'd already survived the demise of one close friendship. I'd survived a lot worse than losing a friend.

But there was still a part of me that held out hope.

"Come on, guys!" Adam yelled as the other team scored a touchdown, pulling them ahead ten to seven. There were less than two minutes left in the game. I knew that Levi wouldn't get any playing time with the score that close. We watched as the time slowly dwindled on the scoreboard to only thirty seconds left. I started to fold the blanket I had on my lap, getting ready to head for the exit.

My attention was drawn back to the field as whistles began to blow. There was some commotion going on and flags being tossed.

"What's going on?" I asked.

Adam surveyed the scene. "Interference or someone's hurt."

As the bodies slowly started to break away from the pile on the field, one player remained. He was on his back and grabbing his knee.

The entire place was silent as the coach and the team trainer ran out and assessed the situation. The players stood by in a vigil-like way, all probably worried about their teammate and also unnerved by the reminder of how fragile our bodies could be.

The crowd started to applaud as the player began to limp off the field, one arm over the trainer.

"Hey, that was Kyle Jankowski," Adam said as he clapped louder.

Poor Kyle, I thought. Then it registered that Kyle was one of the wide receivers.

I looked over and caught Mrs. Rodgers's eye. I didn't know if it was appropriate to be hopeful that Levi would get pulled in at the expense of another player's health. But that was exactly what happened.

Levi started to jog out onto the field.

"GO, LEVI!" Adam shouted loudly, and patted me on the back.

I felt my heart beat faster. But I was sure it was nothing compared to what Levi was going through.

The team lined up and the ball was snapped to Jacob Thomas, the quarterback. He moved back and surveyed the players making their way down the field. Jacob always had more time than most quarterbacks in the district because Keith was his left tackle. No opposing player really had a chance of getting to him with Keith blocking.

Jacob threw the ball long down the field. I held my breath, conflicted about whether I wanted the ball to be thrown to Levi or not. While I wanted him to score, I also didn't want him to drop the ball and be accountable for a loss. Even though I always thought it was unfair that one player was either applauded or vilified if they scored or didn't in the last seconds of a game. The other players on the team were responsible for their getting to that moment. One player does not a team or victory make.

It was an incomplete pass. The team quickly scrambled near the forty-yard line. There were less than twenty seconds on the clock. The ball snapped. Jacob kept shuffling back, looking for an opening. We were at fifteen seconds. The crowd was on its feet. The ball sailed through the air. It was headed straight to Levi, who was running fast toward the end zone.

I swear time stood still for those few seconds. The entire place was silent. Everybody's eyes were following the ball's trajectory.

Levi held his arms out, his focus clear.

He jumped up slightly and caught the ball. He hesitated for a second, probably shocked that the ball was safe in his arms. He turned around and sprinted to the end zone.

The stands erupted in applause while the remaining players arrived in the end zone to celebrate their victory.

Adam and I hugged each other. We hugged the people next to us. I made my way over to Levi's mom and dad.

"That was amazing!" I said as Dr. Rodgers picked me up.

Celebrating with Levi's parents felt right. They were like my family — that hadn't changed. I knew we'd get back to the place we once were. You don't just toss family aside.

I glanced down at the field. Stacey ran over with the other cheerleaders and joined in the commotion. He quickly kissed her before the team hoisted him up.

Levi was beaming. This was all he ever wanted: to be part of a team. One of the guys.

The elation I felt quickly evaporated. While I knew I should be happy for him, I had to face the truth.

I knew right then that I had lost him for good.

It's truly amazing what winning a game can do for someone's confidence. Or ego.

I texted Levi after the game on Friday to congratulate him and never heard back. I saw him in the parking lot at school that Monday morning and gave him a wave, but he was too busy being the athletic stud he'd always dreamed of to notice me.

The entire school kept talking about it as if we'd never won a football game before. Nobody seemed to remember that it had been an extremely boring game for the first three quarters. Apparently, the last twenty seconds were the only thing that mattered. Had that play happened with two minutes left, we would've already moved on to something else.

And yes, I was being a horrible friend for not being more excited for Levi, but were we even friends anymore? We hadn't talked in weeks. He had bigger (in no way better) people to spend his time with.

My annoyance was at an all-time high when I turned the corner on my way from English to see Levi walking with Tim and Keith. They had on their letter jackets and walked down the hallways with that athletic air of superiority that I never quite understood. So you can throw a ball or hit a ball or do something with a ball rather well — that entitles you to some kind of hero worship? The band kids with their musical talents didn't walk around like we should all feel lucky to be graced with their presence.

I reminded myself that only a small percentage of their team would end up playing sports in college, and an even smaller percentage would go on to become professional athletic egomaniacs, if any at all. So at most, Keith would sit around twenty years from now, fat and balding, recounting the glory days of his high school athletic career.

I wanted to believe, at least hope, that my best years were ahead of me. It would be too depressing to fathom if high school was as good as it got.

"Hey, Macallan," Keith sang out to me.

I grimaced as I passed by.

"Oh, it must be someone's time of the month." Keith snickered. "You've got to have that marked on your calendar, right, California? Can't imagine you want to be near her when that hits."

First, *ew*. Second, was that the best Keith could come up with for a reason to not be pleased as punch to talk to him? It couldn't be that he was a complete tool, so it must be a womanly function.

I stopped in the hallway. I should've ignored him and kept going, but I wasn't in the mood for his crap today.

"Is that the best you got?" I spat out.

The three of them stopped, and all of them turned around except Levi. Who muttered something about ignoring me.

Keith smirked at me. "Oh, I've got much more, but I don't think you could handle it."

Keith was used to getting what he wanted. And in that moment, I wanted to get under his skin. To have someone else feel dejected for a change.

"Believe me, Keith, I'm sure I can handle it just fine, since you apparently only know about women from what you find out in health class. So try me."

Tim did that "*oh*" thing guys do when they try to one up each other. "She did *not* just say that." He was laughing. Levi remained motionless.

Keith was not as amused. "Honestly, Macallan, I've so got you outnumbered in terms of intelligence."

That was laughable.

Seeing his smug face infuriated me so much. He'd taken Levi away from me, and I wasn't going to be so easy on him this time.

I leaned in toward him. "You do know that a D on a paper is not for *dope job, yo*, right?"

Keith sized me up, and then a smile slowly spread across his face, like he knew he'd gotten me. But there was no way Keith was going to get me. As a date, in an argument, ever.

"Well, yeah." Then he slurred his voice. "*I'm* not part retard."

I was stunned for a second.

I walked a few steps closer. Levi took a few steps back. "Excuse me — would you care to repeat that?" I was convinced that even Keith wouldn't stoop so low.

He bent his arms up toward his collarbone and let his wrists go limp so his hands were dangling. He collapsed his legs together at the knees and started to walk like he had a disability. "I don't know, can I? What's *repeat* mean?"

Before I could understand my movements, I pushed Keith. Hard. He stepped back a few inches. Then he laughed. Which angered me more.

"Macallan." Levi grabbed my arm. "Calm down."

I shoved him away. "No, I will *not* calm down. And how are you going to stand here like that when he's making fun of my uncle, who, need I remind you, has been nothing but kind to you? Has never said a bad word about anybody? Who certainly would never be so cruel as to make fun of somebody?" My voice started to crack. I could feel my entire body start to shake.

"God." Keith looked shocked at my behavior. "I'm sorry, Macallan. I thought you could take a joke."

"Do you find this funny?" I asked, my voice hard. I didn't want to cry in front of Keith. I could not let him know that he *had* gotten to me. "You're so pathetic. I can't wait to see you in ten years when the reality of life outside these walls hits you."

His face became as hard as my voice. "You think you're so tough and above it all, don't you? But guess what. Just because your mom's dead doesn't mean you can be such a bitch."

A rage I could not describe, one that I hadn't felt in years, overtook my body. Even though I could see that the second those words left his mouth, he regretted them, it was too little, too late. Keith could say what he wanted about me, but how dare he bring up my mom.

I wanted to shut him up. And I did that the only way I knew how.

He wasn't lucky like Levi to get a kiss from me.

Instead, I tightened up my fists and hit him right in the kisser.

Keith, Mr. Athlete Extraordinaire, was knocked onto his butt.

I towered over him. "You say one more word to me ever again about my family, and I will not be so gentle."

I turned on my heel and came face-to-face with Mr. Matthews, the gym teacher.

"Miss Dietz, I think you need to come to the office, and that goes for you gentlemen as well."

"*She* attacked *me*!" Keith cried out.

"That's enough, Mr. Simon." Mr. Matthews stepped in between us. "Don't think I didn't hear what you were saying."

The four of us followed Mr. Matthews to the office. I was put in a separate room from them. I knew I was in trouble. I knew my flawless school record was in jeopardy. But I didn't care. I was angry. I was mad at the world. And why shouldn't I have been? I'd had the most important thing taken away from me without explanation. There were times where I was able to be strong. Many instances where I could pretend that everything was fine.

But sometimes a girl just needs her mother.

The wait in the principal's office felt like forever. I had the entire time to reevaluate how I acted. I remembered once in first grade I'd been mad at this fourth-grade boy who always teased me during recess. He'd call me names and sometimes throw sticks at me.

I finally told Mom about it. I said that I hated him and I wanted to punch him in the face.

Mom said I should never hit anybody, because violence was never the answer. That hitting someone showed that you cared. And you should never give someone that kind of power over you.

But it wasn't Keith I was mad at. Or cared about.

The door finally opened and I saw my father. I felt so guilty for having to bring him in. I never wanted to be responsible for one of those calls.

"Hey, Calley," Dad said softly to me. He only called me this when he was worried about his "baby girl."

Principal Boockmeier motioned for him to sit down. I couldn't even look at my father, I was so horrified by my behavior.

"Well, I filled in your father about what happened. It seems that Levi's and Tim's stories matched. Keith's seemed to be a bit more dramatic." Principal Boockmeier pursed her lips, like she was holding in a laugh. "While I understand you were provoked, what Keith said, though unfortunate, did not warrant your response. We have a very tough policy on violence of any kind, and you did hit him. So you'll be suspended for the rest of the week and have after-school detention for two weeks. If there are no more incidents, this will not go on your college transcripts."

I was shocked and relieved. Thanksgiving was this week, so I was only going to miss two days. And there was a chance it wouldn't totally mess up my record.

I quickly got up and followed Dad out of school. He stayed silent on the car ride home. I looked down at my sore, slightly red right hand.

The car stopped and Dad shut off the engine. I looked up and found us in the Culver's parking lot.

"What . . ." I mumbled.

Dad turned to me, tears in his eyes. "I can't say that was a fun call to get, Macallan. But then I heard from both Principal Boockmeier and Levi about what happened and, well . . . your mother was one of the sweetest people on earth. She wouldn't have hurt a fly."

Tears began to well up in my eyes. I'd let my father down and, worse, I'd let my mother down.

"But" — he put his hand on mine — "she would never have tolerated anybody talking crap about her family. *That* would not go over well. Your mother would've done the same thing, sweetheart. You remind me more and more of her every day, and while I might not be able to help you with everything she could, I'm so proud of you. She would've been, too."

"Really?" Tears were coming out harder now.

"Of course." Dad held on to my hand tightly. "And I know she's looking down on you right now, probably laughing a little, and wishing she could be here with you. She'd want me to treat you to some custard for being strong and standing up for your uncle, and for yourself."

I pictured Mom as Dad described her, and knew he was

right. She'd never tolerated anybody treating Adam differently. One of the things Dad said he loved most about her when they first started dating was that she never babied Adam. She treated his younger brother like everybody else. She certainly wouldn't have allowed anybody to speak to him, or me, that way.

"Is that a smile I'm seeing?" Dad asked.

I nodded. "You're right. I know Mom would be proud. She'd be proud of both of us, Dad." He seemed surprised about my confession, but I wasn't the only person who'd lost somebody. "Let's go get some custard."

I'm so sorry, Macallan. You know how awful I feel about what happened. I should've stepped in, *I* should've punched him in the face. I can't believe I acted like such a wimp. It really is a miracle you ever talked to me again. And I'm grateful that I've never had to experience your right hook.

I'm so sorry, I know I shouldn't joke about that.

I'm such an idiot.

Blimey if I didn't deserve a punch in the face.

I'm so sorry.

Moving on.

CHAPTER FOURTEEN

I needed to clear my head.

So I did the only thing I could think of to make me feel better.

Run.

Since football season was over, I didn't have to worry about running too long and burning off extra calories. Or have to think about keeping my weight up. Or think about anything.

I only had to run.

I'll admit that catching that ball and hearing the cheering was amazing. I understand how people can get caught up in moments like that. How you want to keep reliving one small fraction of time when you felt invincible.

My dad has this friend who always makes him tell this story about a baseball game from back in high school. Every time the guy's over, he tells it. And we sit there like we haven't heard it a million times before. I thought it was pathetic, how you could look back on something so insignificant as one game, one play, and think that was the greatest moment in your life.

But then I totally got it.

I was THE MAN. The hero. The MVP. And all I had to do was catch a ball. One that Jacob threw with precision. Did he get the credit he deserved? Not as much as I did.

There I was on a total ego high when Macallan had to come in and crash the party.

And what did THE MAN, the hero, the MVP do? He stood there terrified and did nothing.

NOTHING.

I had to recount what happened not only to the principal, but to Macallan's dad. He looked so upset when he arrived at school, then had to listen to me tell him how brave his daughter had been.

While I'd just stood there.

I had to tell him all the awful things Keith had said.

While I'd just stood there.

I'd never felt more like a loser in my life.

Before I really knew where I was running to, I ended up at Riverside Park. I'd been running so hard, I could see my breath come out in short spurts. I walked a bit to cool down, even though the cold weather was already helping with that.

I normally didn't run that hard when it was early winter, but I needed to get some distance from what had happened the day before.

I'd begun to walk forward to the swings when I noticed someone stretching, out over by the picnic tables. I abruptly stopped when I realized it was Macallan. She had her right leg up on the table and was bending over to stretch out her hamstrings.

Confusion swirled around whether I should approach her or walk away before she saw me.

I stepped forward. It was about time I started acting like the stud I'd been pretending to be for the past week. Or more accurately, past few months.

"Hey!" I called out to her.

She spun around quickly. "Oh, hey." She paused for a second before continuing to stretch.

"You just starting?"

"Nope, I'm done."

I knew that. I knew her routine. She was happy running for herself. To help clear her head. She didn't need the justification of a team or a crowd to do something.

I had no idea what to do. I wanted to make things right between us, but I wasn't sure at what cost. So I would start with what I should've done months ago: apologize.

"Macallan, about —"

She cut me off. "I don't want to talk about it."

"He's a jerk," I offered.

Her lip curled slightly. "He's your best friend."

I wanted to say *No, he's not. You are.* But I hadn't been acting like a friend to her, let alone a best friend.

I opened my mouth, trying to think of something to say to mend this tension between us. The words that came out were: "See you at Thanksgiving."

See you at Thanksgiving? I should've asked her to punch me right then and there. Maybe she would've knocked some sense into me.

"Yeah." She began to walk away.

"Hey, Macallan," I called after her. "Is it okay that we're still coming?"

She hesitated briefly. "Of course."

While that pause was only a couple seconds, it was long enough for me to know I'd done some real damage.

My parents let me drive my new car to Thanksgiving. I should've been excited for this rather adult responsibility, but I was nervous. For the first time since I've known the Dietzes, I wasn't sure how to act. This needed to be a great Thanksgiving for Macallan. I didn't want to do anything or say anything that would upset her.

What I did want was for us to figure some way to get back to normal. To pre-Levi-being-an-idiot. To pre-Ireland. Maybe even to pre-Emily.

Adam opened the door with a giant smile. "Happy Thanksgiving!"

Guilt stabbed me as I thought about what Keith had said.

We all exchanged holiday greetings and unloaded our winter coats and gifts. We'd brought the centerpiece, pumpkin pie, shrimp for an appetizer, and some adult beverages for the grown-ups.

The amazing smell of the holidays greeted us as we stepped into the living room.

Mom set out the shrimp cocktail on the coffee table next to Macallan's offerings: spiced pecans, bacon roll-ups, and, I was beyond thrilled to see, her cheese ball.

"Yes!" I sat down and grabbed a cracker.

"Get your own!" Adam gently shoved me as we both started helping ourselves to the food. If only Thanksgiving happened in the summer, I would never have had a problem putting on weight for football season.

"Macallan!" Mom greeted Macallan with a giant hug as she entered the room. "This all looks wonderful. What can I help you with?"

"Nothing, really." She glanced at her watch. "I don't have to worry about anything for at least thirty minutes."

"Do you want me to be on turkey duty?" Mom offered.

"Turkey's done. I cooked it yesterday." Macallan popped a bacon roll-up into her mouth. "I did the fancy turkey last time. This year I wanted to do my aunt Janet's recipe. Cooked the turkey yesterday, then marinated it overnight in gravy."

"It's so good," Adam said as he took the knife away from me to help himself to more cheese ball.

"Don't eat the entire cheese ball! You know I've got a ton of food for dinner: stuffing, wild rice, macaroni and cheese, sweet potato casserole, glazed carrots. . . . I think there's a green vegetable some-where in there. I'm not sure, it's a holiday!"

"It all sounds fabulous." Mom rubbed Macallan's arm. "You look gorgeous, sweetie." She really did. She had this green dress on that accentuated her red hair. "We've really missed you. All we keep hear-ing from Levi is how busy you've been."

The cheese ball got caught in my throat. I didn't want the day to begin with me getting caught in a lie. I wanted this to be a fun meal like we always had together, even though I knew my mere presence was enough to prevent that from happening.

I studied Macallan's face to see if she was going to give away the fact that I'd been using excuse after excuse for reasons why Macallan wasn't around. Why we couldn't do Sunday dinners any-more. I kept saying Macallan had this cooking thing or that academic event.

But the real reason was that I was being selfish. I didn't want any-thing to take away from my time with my guys. I didn't want to be attached to Macallan. Like she was some sort of tether weighing me down. But it was my ego, my insecurity about where I fit in that was responsible for my stupidity.

Macallan smiled. "Yeah, it's been a crazy few months." She took a handful of pecans and headed into the kitchen.

"Ah, I'm going to see if she needs any help," I said as I got up. I ignored the sarcastic comments from my dad, as it was pretty clear that the only help I could give anybody in the kitchen would be to exit immediately.

Macallan was washing a pot. Her back was to me. I couldn't tell if she was angry.

"Do you need help?" I offered.

Her shoulders tensed up. "No, I'm okay."

"Are you sure?" I approached the side of the sink and picked up a towel.

"Suit yourself." She handed me the dripping dish.

Macallan jumped up to sit on the kitchen island as I began to dry off the pot.

"Did you invite Stacey for dessert?" she asked.

When Mom had talked to Macallan to see what we could bring, Macallan had invited Stacey to join us later when she was done with her family.

"Nah. I thought it would be good to be only family." I hesitated. "To tell you the truth, I'm not sure how much longer we'll be together." Which was true. Stacey was a cool girl, but I was with her because I thought I should be with a cheerleader. That was what most of the varsity athletes did. That was what Keith did. Plus, I thought it would be easier to have a girlfriend to keep my feelings for Macallan in check. And that wasn't fair to Stacey. Or to me.

"That's too bad," Macallan replied. There was absolutely no emotion on her face. I couldn't tell if she really thought this was bad news or if she was being sarcastic. Usually, it was pretty clear when she was being sarcastic, mostly at my expense.

A smile started to slowly spread across my lips as I thought back on some of our epic bantering sessions. Guys think they can talk crap, but they've got nothing on Macallan in terms of wit and a rapid-fire reflex.

She looked confused. "You're smiling over your relationship ending?"

"No, no." I didn't need her to think of me worse than she probably already did. "I was thinking about the time we went to that Brewers game —"

"And you dropped your hot dog," she finished for me.

"Yes! And you would not let me forget it because I —"

"*Still* ate it!"

"Yeah!" I said a little louder than I intended, mostly because I was excited to remind her about a fun time we'd had. "But!"

"There's no buts about it. It was disgusting."

"It was only —"

" 'On the floor for five seconds.' " She repeated what I kept saying to her that day in a low voice, the one she always used when she imitated me. Usually, it annoyed me when she did that. I was ecstatic to hear it from her now.

"Remember, I hadn't put anything on it yet."

"Which would've been better because then you could've at least wiped the dirty ketchup off."

"Yeah, but you wouldn't stop teasing me about it."

"Because it was disgusting." She said this slowly, like she was talking to a toddler.

I started laughing. For the entire game, anytime something happened, the Brewers struck out or the other team scored, Macallan had leaned forward and said, "Well, they may be losing the game, but at least they didn't eat a dirty hot dog." Or "Wow, that must be tough to swallow, although not as tough as a dirty hot dog."

Macallan studied me. "Well, what about it?"

"What about what?"

She wrinkled her nose. "What about that game?"

"Oh," I said, disappointment seeping through. "It was fun."

"Yeah," she agreed. One of her timers went off. "Well, I think I need to ask you to leave. I don't serve dirty food, and with your luck . . ." She let the words hang there, but I was grateful to have her say something teasing to me. Macallan didn't waste her time, or her barbs, on people she didn't care about.

Now that I think about it, having Macallan as my best friend prepared me for all the trash talking that can happen in the locker room. And the weight room.

"You call that a rep?" Keith taunted Tim as he pushed up the weights on the bench press a week after Thanksgiving.

Tim got up and sat down on the mat next to me while I did leg lifts.

"Let me show you how it's done." Keith laid down on the bench press and started easily pumping the weight up and down.

"Yeah, you only weigh fifty pounds more than me, dude," Tim reminded him.

"Dude, I can't help it if I make everything look good."

I stayed quiet as I worked on strengthening my lower body. Tim started stretching, and asked, "You want to go run some suicides on the court?"

The weather had gotten even colder as Christmas approached, so we'd taken to staying inside to work out. We'd hit the weight room above the gymnasium after Tim was done with basketball practice.

"Yeah, man, sounds good." I got up and grabbed my gym towel.

"That's right, you skinny boys can't handle the pressure, so get out of the kitchen," Keith grunted as he finished his last set.

"That didn't even make any sense." Tim laughed.

"Hey, I'm pumping a lot here. Gotta save everything for the game."

"Nice excuse," I snarked at him.

"What's your problem, California?" Keith got up and came toward me. "You've been acting all weird lately."

I hadn't been acting "all weird." I'd just stopped laughing at Keith's jokes when they weren't funny.

Keith continued. "It's like you get a taste of the good life and then can't handle it anymore. But don't worry, this year will fly by and then we'll be back on the field. Senior year's gonna be awesome. You'll for sure start and we will own this place. No question."

I shrugged. That sounded nice, but I didn't know what price I'd have to pay for it. For the first time, I wasn't so sure it would be worth it.

"I'm telling you" — Keith threw me my water bottle — "track is gonna be a shock to your system. You went from playing in front of hundreds screaming your name, to, like, what? Five people on the benches for a track meet?"

Yeah, but all the important people in my life showed up for that.

It was then I realized that maybe Macallan wouldn't be showing up this year. I wouldn't really blame her. But I'd gotten used to having her there, cheering me on.

She was always there for me when I needed her. I only wished I could say the same for myself.

"I think I know what this is about." Keith sat down and motioned me to join him on the opposite bench. I obliged because that was what I did. "Look, I'm sorry about what happened with your chick friend."

"Macallan," I corrected him.

"Macallan." He sighed when he said her name. "I've apologized to her, which I'm pretty sure she didn't believe even though I was being serious. I practically begged Boockmeier to not suspend her. I snapped — I realize that. I don't know what it is about that girl, but she just gets to you. It's like she doesn't care what anybody thinks about her."

No, I thought, *she just doesn't care what* you *think of her.*

"I don't know." Keith looked thoughtful for a second, then slapped his hands against his knees. "Girls, you know?"

No, I didn't know. Clearly, I had no idea.

But I didn't say any of that. I sat there silently until we headed down to the gym and started running suicide drills.

Tim and I lined up at baseline under the basket. Keith had his stopwatch out and yelled for us to start. I sprinted to the free throw line, then back to the baseline, then to the middle of the court, back to the baseline, to the opposite free throw line, back to the base. I couldn't wait to sprint the full length of the court. That was when I excelled. Tim was only a few paces behind me, but I would make it a greater distance in the long stretches.

I couldn't hear what Keith was yelling or anything. I focused on my next goal, the next place I was to touch down, pivot, and start over again.

I knew I had Tim beat heading toward the opposite baseline. All I needed to do was pivot and run back. I bent down to touch the baseline, but when I pivoted, my lower leg stuck and my upper leg turned. I felt a pop, and before I could process what was going on, I buckled under my own weight and collapsed on the court. An excruciating pain from my knee jolted through my entire body. I grabbed my knee and screamed.

I rocked back and forth, holding my leg.

"Stay still, Levi!" Keith was on his knees next to me. "Just try to relax. Tim went to get Coach."

I couldn't stay still. It hurt too much to lie there. My entire body started to shake.

Something was wrong.

Something was very, very wrong.

What is it about guys and having to out-bench-press or outrun one another? Why does everything have to be a competition?

I don't know — testosterone?

That's your excuse for everything.

It is? Well, does it at least work?

No.

Okay, what about you girls?

What about us, the clearly superior gender?

Yeah, you're not biased.

Of course I'm not. We women are a rational, nonjudgmental breed.

Are you even being serious right now?

What do you think?

You know I sometimes don't know if you're being serious or not.

It's one of the flaws of your kind.

Yes, because girls *never give out mixed signals*.

You are one hundred percent correct. That's got to be a first.

I sometimes don't even know why I bother.

See, guys give up on stuff so quickly.

We do not.

Oh, really, do I need to remind you of why we're even talking right now? Who was the bigger person?

Ugh. You're right.

I know.

Girls.

Yes, we are made of awesome.

CHAPTER FIFTEEN

I had finally come face-to-face with my nemesis. And this time I was determined to be the victor.

I gently took the ramekin out of the oven. The soufflé was properly puffed up and looked to be the right consistency. I cradled it in my hand as I cautiously stepped to where my dad was sitting.

"It looks perfect," he remarked once I set it down.

"Taste it," I ordered. This was the fourth soufflé I'd attempted to make. My first two tries hadn't risen since I hadn't beaten the egg whites enough. The third time, I'd taken it out of the oven too soon and it had collapsed before I could even place it on the counter.

Dad smiled as he dived in. I leaned in as he took his first bite.

My phone began to ring. I let it go to voice mail.

"So good," Dad said with a full mouth. He took another gigantic bite.

His phone rang and we both stared at it.

"Who is it?" I asked, afraid something was wrong with Uncle Adam. I snapped up my phone and saw it was Levi's mom right as Dad said it was her.

"Hello?" Dad answered. His face immediately went into a frown. "Oh no — what happened?"

My stomach fell. I tried to decipher what was going on by Dad's expression and his "oh no" and "of course" interjections. Finally he said, "We'll be right over."

"What's going on?" I asked.

"Levi tore his ACL during his workout." Dad shook his head. "They just got back from the hospital and he's pretty upset. Poor guy. We need to go over there now."

"Oh." Levi was always so careful about warming up and not overworking himself. I couldn't believe he'd hurt himself. And that was the kind of injury that takes a really long time to heal. "Doesn't he need rest?"

"Yes, but he was asking for you." Dad got up and grabbed his keys.

"He was?"

Dad turned around to look at me. "Of course, Macallan. You're his best friend." He shook his head like I was being silly. He was already in the garage before I got my senses about me. I quickly pulled out a bag of brownies from the freezer to bring. Mom always said it was polite to bring something over to someone's house. I hadn't been at Levi's house for so long, I almost felt like I was a guest.

So much for being the best friend.

Levi's dad looked so tired when he answered the door.

"I'm so glad you're here." He gave me a tight embrace. "You're the first person he asked for."

I almost said "thanks" but realized that maybe it wasn't the right response. So I decided to ask how Levi was doing.

Dr. Rodgers sighed, the worry openly displayed on his face. "He's obviously upset. We're going to reevaluate it in a week, but he'll most likely need surgery. The tear in his anterior cruciate —" He stopped himself. "Sorry, it's hard to not be a doctor in these instances. Basically, he'll be laid up for a while. The physical therapy alone takes months. He won't be back to normal for at least six months after surgery."

I started to do the math in my head. He would miss track in the spring. Football next year was questionable. So much of his identity rode on his being on a team. At least he should be okay for his last year of track.

We walked into the kitchen and saw Mrs. Rodgers sitting with Keith and Tim at the table. Keith smiled at me, then froze when he saw my dad.

"Hey, guys," I said to relieve the tension.

Dad stood silently next to me. "It's okay," I whispered to him. It was already pretty obvious that I knew how to handle myself around Keith. If anybody should be worried, it should be him.

Keith stood up uncomfortably. "It was pretty bad," he said. Tim nodded in agreement. "And I swear, Macallan, it wasn't my fault."

"Why would I think it was your fault?" I said. Although the thought *had* crossed my mind.

He let out a slight grunt. "Um, it's pretty clear you don't like me."

"Whatever would've given you that impression?" I asked dryly.

"Macallan," Levi's dad interrupted. "He's upstairs and ready to see you."

I walked up the stairs slowly, unsure of what was waiting for me in Levi's room. Even though the door was open, I knocked on it anyway.

He was sitting up in bed, his right leg wrapped up, elevated, and with a pack of ice on it.

"How you feeling?" I asked, even though his face gave away his misery.

"I can't believe how much I messed this up." He leaned his head back and closed his eyes.

"It's going to be okay." I grabbed his desk chair and brought it over to his bedside. "You'll get stronger from this."

"Six months. At least." His voice revealed that he could hardly believe it himself. His eyes darted to my side. "What is that?" He gestured at the bag of brownies I had forgotten all about. I was gripping it as if my life depended on it.

"Oh, um, do you want some brownies? They still need to thaw." I had never felt like a bigger idiot in my life.

He laughed. "It's good to know that some things never change." He winced slightly and I bolted up.

"Are you okay? Do you need something?" I was so worried that he was going to break on my watch.

"No." He looked down at his leg. "Well, I do need a lot. You wouldn't happen to have a spare ACL lying around, by any chance?"

I was relieved he was making a joke. Not that I found any of this funny, but it was nice he wasn't so far gone that his sense of humor had disappeared.

We both sat in silence for a few minutes. I really didn't know what to say to him. To be honest, I'd been waiting for him to apologize to me for months. And I almost told him right then and there that all he needed to do was say he was sorry and mean it. But I knew it wasn't the right time.

I saw it was getting late, and more as an excuse to break the silence, I got up. "I figure you need some —"

He grabbed my arm. "I'm sorry, Macallan."

In my head, I'd planned to list all the reasons he should be sorry and remind him of all the times I had been there for him. Of how hurtful his actions and words had been. Of how much pain he'd caused me. But I didn't need to say any of that.

Because he already knew.

Instead, I said what we both needed to hear.

"It's okay." I leaned down and kissed him on the forehead.

"It's not," he said. "What I did —"

I stopped him. "I know, and you've apologized. And I'm sorry, too. What I think we both need is to get back to where we used to be."

"That's all I want." He smiled at me. That familiar smile I hadn't seen on his face in months. "You know I don't deserve you."

"Oh, I do know." I winked at him, then turned and walked downstairs. I had a feeling that things were going to be okay between us.

We had both made mistakes and been admittedly stubborn, but we needed to move on with, not away from, each other.

"Hey!" Dad lit up when he saw me. "You're smiling. I take it everything's okay up there."

I knew, given the circumstances, my joy should've been more contained, but I couldn't help it.

Levi was in my life again.

The weeks leading up to Christmas were busier than usual.

On top of studying for exams, Christmas shopping, and booking extra babysitting gigs to pay for said shopping, I also had to be Levi's caretaker at school. I was given keys to his car so I could help his mom transport him to and from school. I also helped him with his bags, which really annoyed him more than the crutches he had to use until his surgery, which was scheduled for two days after New Year's.

Keith, Tim, and the other guys on the team were helpful for the first few days, but either their guilt had subsided or the luster of helping out their fellow man lessened, because they pretty much became MIA. Sure, they'd cheer "California" when they saw Levi hobbling in the hallway, but that was the extent of their help.

Of course Stacey and the cheerleaders (even Emily) were more than willing to help. Nothing like playing Florence Nightingale to drum up romantic delusions.

Unfortunately, Levi was not an appreciative patient. He hated asking the guys for help and didn't want to be pitied by any of the girls. He especially despised having his mom come into school with him, because it made him feel like he was in first grade again.

That left me. I was sure he wasn't thrilled he had to rely on me so much, but I never put up with his crap. So we got on nicely.

"I can do it myself," he said one day before lunch as I was opening his locker.

"Suit yourself." I backed away and watched him balance on one leg and maneuver his crutches so he could open his locker. Once he got the lock open, he had to hop back to make room for the door to swing open. One of the crutches fell as he tried to grab his lunch bag.

Luckily, I was anticipating this and grabbed it before it hit the floor.

"You know, I can make your lunch and bring it with me — it's not a big deal," I offered.

"I can do this," he mumbled.

I teased him. "Oh, poor you, I'm offering to make you lunch. You love my food."

Danielle approached us. "Wait, are you offering to cook? What does a girl need to do to get some of your chicken salad?"

"Injure yourself," Levi snapped.

I shook my head at Danielle. "He's having one of those days."

"Don't talk about me like I'm not here," Levi groaned.

"Come on." I grabbed his lunch, and the three of us walked

to the cafeteria. "If you're going to be like this all day, we can have you sit somewhere else."

"Sorry," he said quietly. "I don't meant to be —"

I graciously finished the sentence for him. "Stubborn. Ungrateful. Gloomy. A pain in the rear."

"Yes." A smile began to warm his face. "All of that and more."

I set his lunch down, took his crutches from him, and leaned them against the wall. "At least you acknowledge that. And, of course, how awesome I am."

"Of course." He smiled as he opened his lunch bag. "How could I ever forget?"

"I honestly don't know." I rested my chin on my hand. "How did you?"

Danielle groaned. "It's amazing how quickly you two snap back into place. It's almost sickening, really."

"Levi just needs a constant reminder of how much he needs me." I knew this always got under Levi's skin, even though it was kind of the truth. I only teased him about it because he seemed to prefer it when I made fun of him.

Typical boy.

"So what's the plan for break?" Danielle asked. We only had a few days left before Christmas.

"I'm thinking some sloth combined with gluttony." I was so tired from studying and carting around Levi. I was looking forward to ten days of doing nothing but watching TV, reading, and stuffing my face. I'd asked Dad for some new cookbooks and was going to try making sushi from scratch.

(Starting with California rolls — there was no need to spend the holidays with food poisoning.)

"Ah, sloth and gluttony." Danielle smiled. "Two of the greatest words in the English language."

I turned toward Levi. "You invited Stacey to New Year's, right?" Since Levi wasn't in the mood to go to any party, I volunteered to cook a big meal that night. Danielle was coming, but leaving early to go to a band party.

He nodded. "Yeah, although I don't want her to not have a good time because of me."

"Hey!" I slapped my hand against the table. "Speak for yourself, but I'm a very fun time."

"Yeah," Danielle agreed, "read the stalls in the guy's bathroom."

"Ha, ha." I shot her a dirty look.

I didn't really understand Levi's relationship with Stacey. I'd thought they were breaking up, but they were still together. And I didn't fault him for that. She was one of those gorgeous, bubbly girls who's always smiling and giving out compliments. It seemed like a nice, easy relationship for Levi. Not a lot of complications. And I'm an expert on Levi and complications. So I honestly had no idea why he didn't want to spend more time with her, even though he was claiming it was for her sake. It seemed like he was always making excuses to not hang out with her. And why on earth would he not want her to be around on New Year's Eve? His track record of girlfriends being faithful on that day was not great. But he didn't need me to remind him of it.

Plus, I had learned my lesson. I knew better than to stick my nose in Levi's relationships. If he wanted to talk to me about it, fine. But I wasn't getting involved.

Things never worked out when I did.

Given the craziness that preceded it, Christmas was fairly uneventful. Which I was more than happy with.

Since both Stacey and Danielle were leaving New Year's Eve supper early to go to other parties, it seemed Levi and I would be ringing in the New Year in a very quiet, very unexciting way.

Stacey was wearing a festive minidress and black leggings with silver sparkles. Her hair was pulled back in a silver headband. Levi had on jeans and a sweatshirt. Even Danielle, who was going to hang out with a few other friends after hanging out with us, was wearing a skirt. I did make *some* effort and wore nice dark jeans and a black wrap sweater with purple sequins.

"Hey, Adam!" Levi greeted my uncle, who was sitting on the couch. "I didn't realize we were going to have a chaperone. Better cancel the keg!"

Adam laughed. "Yeah, right."

"I'm surprised you aren't breaking hearts tonight, Adam!" Levi teased.

Adam blushed. The ladies certainly loved him; he was a charmer.

"He's staying for supper, then heading off," I said. It seemed that everybody had somewhere else to be. Even Dad was over at Levi's house for their party. I was invited to a couple places but turned them down. Levi wasn't interested in going far in his condition, although he didn't want to stay at home and have all his parents' friends fuss over him. His surgery was in a couple days, so he was understandably in a solemn mood.

The five of us settled down at the dining room table. I didn't want to go too fancy tonight because I wasn't sure what kind of food Stacey liked and Levi was no help. I did a basic chicken Caesar salad, ricotta gnocchi with creamy pesto sauce, bruschetta, and baked Alaska for dessert.

"Oh, wow!" Stacey exclaimed with a full mouth. "This is SO good."

All right, maybe I'd wanted to impress her just a little.

"So," Danielle said to me as she rubbed her tummy, "I think I have to end our friendship if I want to fit into my dress for the winter dance."

"It's six weeks away," I reminded her.

"Oh, I'm only taking a break." She eyed the remaining piece of baked Alaska in the center of the table. "I plan on stuffing my face more. I can start worrying about the dance next year." She glanced at her watch. "I've got less than four hours."

"Do you know who you're going with?" Stacey asked Danielle.

Danielle raised her eyebrows. "There's a certain drummer that I have my eye on."

"Uh-oh," I teased. "You know what they say about drummers?"

"That they have excellent rhythm," Danielle deadpanned.

"No." Levi looked at me. "That's not it. Could you remind me, Macallan?"

"Oi, they're so chuffed because they can bang a drum . . ." I started.

Levi graciously continued. "I been bangin' on me table since I was a wee one. Where's me groupies?"

"Dodgy, drummers are."

Levi then delivered the punch line. "Blimey if I haven't been bangin' me head listenin' to you lot."

Danielle looked at the two of us. "Does anybody *ever* have any clue what you two go on and on about?"

"I do," Levi and I said in unison.

Danielle looked at Stacey. "We should get out of here before *I* start banging my head."

Not surprisingly, Danielle and Stacey left for their respective parties instead of hanging out with me and Levi. Adam stayed a while to help me with the dishes since Levi needed to rest his leg. Adam also helped me get Levi down to the basement so he could lie on the sectional's chaise lounge.

"You need anything else?" Adam asked.

"I think we're good." I gave him a big hug. He high-fived Levi and then left us alone.

"Now, is there anything else I could get you?" I bowed down as if he was my master.

"It's about time I get some respect from you." He then gestured for me to twirl around.

"In your dreams."

"Hey, it couldn't hurt to ask."

"I wouldn't press your luck on that." I lifted up a pillow and pretended to hit him.

"You wouldn't hurt a man who's in such a delicate condition, would you?" He stuck out his lip in a pout.

"You don't know me very well."

His eyes lit up. "Actually, I do. Could you hand me my bag?"

I obliged.

Levi dug around the duffel. "I have a surprise for you." He then presented a DVD of the *Buggy and Floyd Christmas Special*.

"Where did you get this?" I knew it had aired in the UK a couple weeks ago, but I had no idea when it was coming stateside.

"I have connections."

I tore open the case and put the disc in. "Did you watch it?"

"No way. Not without you."

I didn't know if I would've had the same willpower.

I curled up on the couch next to Levi. We both began singing the *Buggy and Floyd* theme song at the top of our lungs.

"Gah! I'm so excited!" I reached out to playfully punch Levi but stopped myself, not wanting to actually hit a man while he was down.

The special was an hour long, so we got double the Buggy. It was a surprisingly poignant episode. Generally, Floyd was getting Buggy out of whatever wild fiasco he'd gotten himself into. But within the first five minutes, Floyd left Buggy. "I can't take your tomfoolery!" he exclaimed.

"Who's Tom and who's he foolin'?" Buggy replied, to the laughter of the studio audience.

"You're a grown man, Theodore." Floyd used Buggy's proper name for the first time I could remember. "It's time you act like it." And he walked out.

"Wow," I exclaimed. "I can't believe Floyd did that." I knew they were fictional characters, but this was so unlike them. I wasn't sure if I wanted to keep watching. I liked my memories of them as the funny, quarreling duo.

"I know," Levi said in a quiet voice. "I mean, it's a miracle Floyd didn't do it sooner. He can be so crotchety."

I paused the DVD. "Did you just use the word *crotchety*?"

"Ah, yeah." He looked at me incredulously. "All Floyd does is complain about Buggy and pretty much all of society. He's always making little comments about how he doesn't understand the way certain things are. Sure, it's funny, but the fact he's had enough of it isn't that surprising."

"You have to admit that Floyd has a point most of the time."

Levi started laughing. "Oh my God. Yes! How am I only seeing this now?"

"Seeing what?"

He pointed at me. "You're Floyd!"

"I'm *what*?" My mouth was open. I couldn't believe Levi was comparing me to some *crotchety* old British man.

"You're always making these observations like 'Why does Keith think he's superior just because he can tackle a guy?'"

"That's a valid observation," I defended.

"And 'Why do people say L-O-L — aren't they supposed to be laughing? Have we become that lazy of a society?'"

"Like that doesn't drive you crazy."

Levi was really laughing now. "It all makes sense why you like this show so much."

"So does this make you Buggy?" I shot back.

"Well, he *is* hilarious."

"He's also a complete bumbling fool, so I guess . . ." I sank back in the seat.

"Okay, okay." Levi grabbed the remote from me. "We'll put the show back on. Don't want to get your old-man undies in a bunch."

This time I did hit him.

"Ouch." He rubbed his shoulder.

"Blimey if I could help it." I gave him a goofy grin before turning back to the TV.

We watched as Buggy and Floyd struggled without each other. It hit close to home in a way. Buggy was caught in the rain while a depressing song played as he roamed around aimlessly. I started to feel tears sting the back of my eyes. I couldn't believe an episode of *Buggy and Floyd* was going to make me cry.

Floyd rounded the corner with a large gold umbrella. He paused as he saw his former best friend. He walked slowly toward him.

Levi grabbed my hand.

Floyd covered Buggy with his umbrella.

"It's London," Floyd said. "You know you need a brolly year-round."

Buggy smiled shyly at him. "You're right. Blimey if —" He stopped himself.

Was this the end of Buggy's punch line? Levi and I exchanged a look.

Buggy continued. "No, what I *want* right now is a brolly to shield me from the rain. But what I *need* is me best friend."

Floyd put his arm around Buggy. "Blimey if I could've said it better me self."

They headed back to their flat to open Christmas presents. There were a few more comical moments, but the entire episode left me reflective, pondering the difference between what you *want* and what you *need*.

Levi and I sat in silence for a few minutes while the credits played.

"Well." Levi finally spoke. "That was unexpected. It was sort of deep."

"Yeah," I agreed. "It was good, though."

"It was . . ." Levi stared off into the distance.

I turned on the TV to watch the countdown to the New Year. We made small talk about the various singers and actors on TV.

Then it came to the countdown. Levi and I held out glasses of sparkling cider and clinked as confetti rained down in New York City.

"Happy New Year!" I leaned over and gave him a hug.

"Happy New Year!" His smile quickly vanished. "Hey, Macallan?"

Something about the tone of his voice set me on edge. "Yeah?"

"Do you want — I mean, do you need me to take you to the winter dance?"

That wasn't what I was expecting. Although I really didn't know what I should've expected.

"You know how I feel about high school dances."

He smiled. "I certainly do, Floyd."

I glared at him. "I don't *need* to go."

"Okay, but do you *want* to go?"

I nodded. "Sure, but I'm not going to go for the sake of going. If I find someone I want to go with, I'll go. If I don't, the sun will still rise the next day."

"But I made you that promise," he reminded me.

The promise. The one we made before high school about not letting one of us attend a function alone. That lasted for the first half of the year, then I started seeing Ian, and Levi started seeing Carrie. Then we weren't really speaking. And now he was with Stacey.

"It's okay," I said. Because it was. Would I have fun with Levi at the dance? Of course. But that wouldn't be fair to Stacey.

"Macallan?" Levi leaned toward me. "What *do* you want?"

It seemed like a simple question, but it wasn't. With our history, it was as charged as a stick of dynamite. One wrong move and *boom* — our friendship would be in pieces.

Was this really a conversation we should be having when he was so vulnerable and I was so . . . ? I didn't know what I was, besides confused.

"I know what I want." I stood up. Levi looked expectantly. "Pie, I want some pie."

I went upstairs. I studied my face in the kitchen window. I knew better. We both did.

We had both been burned before. There was no way I was going to play with that fire.

Do you know why I didn't kiss you at midnight?

Because you valued your life?

That. *And* I didn't know what you'd do. Probably run away to the Arctic.

You're never going to let me live that down, are you?

Let me think. . . . Nope.

Figures.

Yeah, well, at least I have this one thing over you.

True.

And you have so much over me.

That's because of your actions, not mine.

Whatever, Floyd.

Oh, you're going to pay for that.

I have no doubt.

CHAPTER SIXTEEN

Oddly enough, starting off a new year with knee surgery wasn't as bad an omen as I'd originally thought. I did get to miss the first week back at school, so no complaints from me on that one.

Sure, I was a huge pain after my injury because I was *in* so much pain. I went through my five stages of grief: I was mad, then upset, followed by angry, which blossomed into frustration, which eventually turned into depression.

But then Macallan came along, as she so often had, and wouldn't put up with any of it. If I complained, she wouldn't let up until I either got over myself or laughed. She carted me back and forth to school. Helped me with my books, cooked for me, did everything I needed, and she didn't complain once. Unless, of course, *I* complained. Which was often.

There was something about her help that calmed me. I didn't like having my mom fret over me. I didn't want Dad to think I was soft, even though he understood the severity of my injury more than anybody. And I hated thinking that the guys felt they had to take care of me.

Oh, yeah, and Stacey. I liked having her around, but things with Macallan were different.

For a second, on New Year's Eve, I thought she was going to tell me that what she wanted was me. That she wanted to kiss me. She only paused for a couple seconds, but in that short amount of time, I managed to get my hopes up to a ridiculous height.

She was one of the last people I saw before I was put under for my surgery, and one of the first people I saw when I woke up. She took the day off school to be with my parents and me. She brought me my homework all week and did these hilarious reenactments of stories involving my friends.

She even took me to physical therapy. Which I was grateful for, because physical therapy sucked. It hurt. It was the most frustrating thing ever. I had to relearn how to use my knee. Something as simple as bending was painful and difficult. If Mom had been there, she would've been worried by the pain I was going through.

But Macallan stood there and helped me when I needed her. She did her homework while my therapist was working on me. And she gave me the strength to not give up, throw a fit, or cry. Which I wanted to do on a daily basis.

After a particularly painful session, Macallan sat next to me during my ice and stim.

"How you feeling?" she asked.

"Better," I lied.

Kim, my therapist, set up my stim machine. "He had a good day today. I have total faith that he'll only be in his brace at the dance in a couple weeks."

"That's great!" Macallan gave me a big smile.

Kim patted her on the shoulder. "You may need him to lean on you more when you dance, but you know how boyfriends can be."

Macallan gave Kim a puzzled look. "Um, yeah, but Levi and I aren't . . ."

"Oh!" Kim looked at both of us. "I thought, um, I didn't mean . . ."

How often had this happened to us? Too often to count. It made sense that Kim would think Macallan was my girlfriend. I'd told her that I had a girlfriend, I'd talked about Macallan a lot, Macallan was always here with me. But I racked my brain trying to think if I had brought up Stacey by name. Surely, I couldn't have neglected to mention her name.

"Sorry," I apologized to Macallan. Like it was my fault that people always assumed we were together. But maybe it was.

She shrugged it off. "It's okay. Maybe if you'd let Stacey come with you . . ."

I knew I was an awful boyfriend to not let Stacey help me. But I liked having this time with Macallan.

"Anyway" — she sat upright — "today was pretty epic at lunch. Keith was all 'me want food, me hate food in cafeteria, me deserve better.'" Whenever Macallan imitated Keith, she pretended he was a Neanderthal, which maybe wasn't far from the truth. She hunched over and stuck out her jaw. "Then Emily was like 'Oh. My. Gawd. You're, like, a picky eater for someone who thinks pizza is a vegetable.'" And whenever she pretended to be Emily — or any girl, really — she put on a Valley Girl accent, twirled her hair, and made her eyes really wide.

It was incredibly entertaining and made the silliest high school encounter hilarious. It was better than actually being there.

"You're such a Mean Girl," I teased.

"Hey, I'm telling it like it is."

"So what else happened today?" I asked. I was heading back to school on Monday and wasn't really looking forward to it, even though I knew it would be good for me to have some normalcy again. I couldn't continue to live in my Macallan bubble, no matter how much I wished I could.

She hesitated. "Well, actually . . ." She bit her lip; it seemed like she was a little nervous. "You know Alex Curtis?"

Alex Curtis? He'd graduated the year before. He'd been on the basketball team, and was really good. We'd hung out a few times this summer before he'd headed off to Marquette.

"Yeah," I said, harsher than I meant to sound. Alex was a good guy, but I didn't want Macallan to think so.

"Well, I ran into him a couple days ago and we were talking, and, um, our moms were good friends." I could tell Macallan was stalling. "Yeah, so he's going to be around for the dance and offered to take me."

Macallan was going to the winter dance with a college guy? A college guy she apparently had a history with? A college guy she'd talked to a couple days ago without mentioning it to me?

"Cool" was the only lame response I could come up with.

Relief flashed across her face. "Yeah, he's really nice. And I didn't even think about the dance when we were talking, but he brought it up. He asked who I was going with and when I said nobody, he . . ." Her cheeks flushed. "He said it was an egregious crime, which he felt it necessary to correct."

She giggled.

I wanted to barf.

"You like him, right?" she asked.

Did I think Alex Curtis was a good guy? Sure.

Did I want to punch Alex Curtis in the face at that exact moment in time? You betcha.

Why couldn't I tell her that? Why couldn't I just tell her how I felt? Why did I fight something I wanted — no, something I *needed* so badly?

But then I flashed to Macallan leaving after I'd confessed my feelings for her. How awkward she'd been when she first came back from Ireland. How I hadn't wanted to drive her away.

But maybe things were different now?

I opened my mouth, daring myself to finally man up. "Macallan."

"Yeah?"

The buzzer on my stim machine went off. Kim came over to remove the ice and pads.

"Levi?" Macallan looked at me with concern. "Was there something you wanted?"

"Never mind."

Time was up.

I began to focus on what I did have: A wonderful family. An awesome best friend. A group of guy friends. And a girlfriend.

That was what I needed to concentrate on.

Stacey insisted on having some people over the Saturday night before my, as Keith had put it, "legendary return to South Lake High School."

"There's my bro," Keith greeted me now, gently putting me into a headlock. "Dude, we missed you at school. Who else am I going to cheat off during trig?"

I smiled and played the part of the happy guest of honor. When I maneuvered my crutches and leg brace to the closest couch, Stacey sat down next to me.

"What can I get you?" she asked. "Do you want something to drink or eat?"

"Just some water, thanks." I knew I was being grumpy, but I was on some serious painkillers, and even soda made my stomach woozy.

Stacey got up to get me some water. I watched her move across the room, greeting everybody, being the perfect hostess.

I realized there was a line of people there to talk to me. I felt like it was a funeral for my football career, with people offering their condolences. Even though the guys kept telling me I'd be fine, I was the one who was speaking to the doctors. They'd confirmed it was going to take several months to get back to somewhat normal, and even then it would be hard for me to pivot and switch directions easily. The best hope I had for senior year was track. Running straight *should* be fine. At least I hoped it would be.

I was itching to run so I could clear my mind. And if there was a time in my life when I needed to get focused, work out issues, it was now.

I smiled politely and thanked everybody who came up to me and told me they hoped I felt better and that I'd be back to running in no time.

All I could do was sit there. Stacey had disappeared, probably talking to someone else in the kitchen.

I really needed that glass of water.

"Hey there," Macallan said, setting a glass of water and a plate of brownies on the end table. She sat down next to me. "Enjoying your audience?"

"Oh, I am so happy to see you."

"You're happy to see my brownies."

I'd been hesitant when Stacey brought up the idea for the party. In the middle of me giving her reasons for why it wasn't a good idea (I wouldn't be up to it, I didn't want people feeling sorry for me, they'd see me in a few days, I didn't want a big deal made out of it), she cut me off with "Macallan will be there. She thinks it's a great idea." She didn't say it in a way that led me believe she resented Macallan. She had always understood about my relationship. She knew how things were with us.

Well, she didn't know *everything* about us.

But Macallan knew Stacey loved her double-fudge brownies.

"This is fun." Macallan tried to cheer me up.

"I guess."

"Oh, *pardon me*." She sighed exaggeratedly. "Everybody wanted to get together to celebrate that your surgery went well, and they're happy to see you. It must be *so* hard to get up in the morning."

"Actually, it *is* hard to get up in the morning." I gestured at my leg brace.

She stood up. "I think I'm going to talk to anybody or anything that isn't so negative. That wall looks tempting."

I reached out my hand. "Please don't go."

Stacey came bounding for the couch. "You made it!" she said to Macallan.

"Yeah, I brought you these." Macallan gestured to the brownies. I grabbed two more before Stacey took the plate.

"Yu-um!" Stacey exclaimed. "Thanks so much!"

"You're welcome."

They looked at each other, neither sure what to say next.

"Um . . ." I stammered.

"Hey!" Stacey said brightly to Macallan. "I hear you're going to the dance with Alex. That's so cool!"

"Yeah, it should be fun," Macallan offered.

"Awesome!" Stacey looked like she was going to explode from either happiness or nerves. I could never read her right.

"Is that food?" Keith came over, then stopped in his tracks when he noticed Macallan next to me.

"Macallan made brownies!" Stacey exclaimed. She held them out to Keith, who clearly had no clue what to do next.

"Relax," Macallan said. "I didn't poison them."

He took a bite.

Macallan continued. "However, I knew you'd be eating them, so I put in a secret ingredient. . . ."

Keith stopped chewing.

Macallan stood up and faced Keith. Every nerve in my body was on edge.

She shook her head. "Keith, I work too hard on my food to waste it on you. Plus" — she leaned in so she was only inches from his face — "you and I both know I don't need to bake to do damage."

She turned on her foot and went to the kitchen.

Keith was flustered. "Man, that girl. She just . . . I think I'd be madly in love with her if she didn't scare me so much. But maybe that's why I like her. Not like I *like* like her." Keith gave up trying to make sense of what happened and walked away, first toward the kitchen, then thinking better of it and heading in the opposite direction.

Stacey laughed. "Wouldn't they make a fun couple?"

I came so close to blurting out, *Wouldn't they WHAT?* but stopped myself.

Apparently my disgust was evident without words. "Calm down!" Stacey's eyes were wide. "I was just joking."

The doorbell rang and Stacey excused herself, leaving me alone at a party that was in my honor.

I thought about what Keith had said. About how Macallan scared him.

I knew exactly what he meant. Because she also scared me.

She scared me *because* I loved her.

On a scale from one to ten, how much of a pain was I after my injury? And please be honest.

Do you think I would hold back on you?

Unfortunately, no.

On a scale from one to ten? Thirteen.

Fair enough.

Now I have a question for you. On a scale from one to ten, how annoyed were you that I was going to the dance with someone else?

Infinity.

CHAPTER SEVENTEEN

It's funny how quickly your opinion of a dance can change.
I always thought the idea of a winter dance was silly. It was only three months after homecoming and three months before prom — did we really need another reason to fret over dates, dresses, and the drama that follows such occasions?

But when a cute college guy asked me to go? Well, who was I to stand in the way of tradition? Plus, we all know how much I loved my distractions.

Alex took me out to eat the weekend before the dance. It was a nice change to have a guy pick me up instead of my having to constantly take Levi around. While I was more than happy to help him out, it was still a chore.

I kept glancing over my menu at Alex. He was only a couple inches taller than me, but he was lean, with broad shoulders, dark hair, and dark eyes — almost the exact opposite of Levi. I couldn't understand why he would want to hang out with me, a high school girl.

"Hey." Alex smiled at me. "Do you remember when we were little and we went up to Door County with our moms?"

My heart warmed at the memory. Our moms had been really close. So, in a way, Alex was my first guy friend. My warm-up to Levi.

"Yes, but as I remember, you weren't that excited to be hanging out with a girl. Ew!" I scrunched up my face.

"That's because I was an idiot."

I did remember that week in Door County when I was six and Alex was eight. We'd gone swimming, went for walks among the cherry trees, and picked our own cherries — our hands and mouths stained red, our bellies full.

"I remember your mom had this *huge* hat." He held his arms out wide. "That hat was *epic*."

That hat. I can still picture her in that black and white striped hat. It flopped nearly over her shoulders.

"Well, Mom and I have the same pasty white skin tone. Don't you remember how burned I got?"

"Yes!" He shook his head. "Your mom took you outside and sprayed you with vinegar."

"That stung so much! But it was better the next day." I'd smelled for a bit, but once the vinegar had evaporated from my skin, it hadn't been so awful. "Mom had some strange home remedies, but they worked."

Alex looked at me thoughtfully. "Is it okay that we talk about her?"

"Of course." I knew it would be a disservice if I didn't celebrate the time I'd had with her.

At least that was the attitude I tried to have. I still would have my moments when I'd get sad. But I would've been worried if that hadn't happened.

Alex got quiet. "I'm sorry we didn't hang out much after."

Alex's mom had joined the parade of casseroles after the funeral. She'd come by every now and then to check up on me, but then life happened. People got busy.

A smile spread across his face. "I do remember being shocked the first time I saw you freshman year. It was like, 'Is that little Macallan Dietz? She's all grown up!'"

I recalled passing Alex in the hallway a few times, and how we'd smile and say hi to each other. But the first time we'd had a real conversation in years was when he spotted me in line at the grocery store.

Alex continued. "And then I couldn't believe you had that boyfriend. What was his name — Lewis?"

"Levi?"

"Yeah, Levi. He's a great runner. But of course, if your relationship ended badly, he's the devil." I had to hand it to Alex — he understood girls very well.

"No, nothing really ended." A look of concern flashed on Alex's face. "Because we never dated. We're just friends. Well, not *just* friends. He's my best friend. He has been for almost five years." Give or take a few months of cold feet and cold shoulders.

"Oh." Alex looked confused.

I was honestly so tired of this conversation that I looked down at the menu and pretended to be really interested in the specials listed.

"Do you know what you want to get?" Alex asked. Probably also grateful to change the subject.

"I think so. Do you want to get cheese curds to start?"

He wrinkled his nose in disgust. "Yuck. I know, how very un-Wisconsin of me, but I don't like those things."

"Oh, okay."

"But feel free to get some."

Usually, Levi and I would split the appetizer, so it would be too much for only me. Even if I did like my fried cheese.

Alex reached into his pocket for his phone. "Sorry — I keep getting texts from my buddies. They're giving me grief for going back to my high school for a dance." He scrolled down his messages, occasionally groaning. "Something about robbing the cradle. How original."

I wasn't going to lie and say I hadn't wondered the same thing. Why would he want to go back to attend a high school dance. Was it pity? Nostalgia? I had no clue. Maybe this was getting more complicated than I thought it would be. I only wanted to go to a dance with a cute boy. And not think of Levi.

But the problem was that Levi always came up.

I tried to convince myself that this dance was nothing. I wanted to go with someone and hope my feelings for Levi would go away.

But they weren't going away. They were growing more and more by the day.

And there was nothing I could do to stop it.

I was conflicted. I felt sick to my stomach.

And I really wanted those cheese curds.

I tried to push everything out of my head the week leading up to the dance.

It was only a dance. I had made plenty of comments about how high school dances were silly and conformed to the ever-sexist stereotype about male-female relationships (it *was* very Floyd of me). And for the first time since homecoming last year, Levi and I both would be going with a date. Him with his girlfriend of nearly six months. Just the thought of seeing his arms around her . . .

It was pretty clear who was winning this battle.

Even though it wasn't a competition.

But part of me felt like it was. Which one of us could survive without the other? And while Levi needed my help to physically get around, he didn't *need* need me.

Well, he did need me to help him pick out a tie.

There I was in his bedroom, a few hours before the dance. He held out two tie options for me.

"I know this is boring," I said, "but I like the skinny black one. It's more formal."

He tossed the other tie aside. "Thanks." He used both his arms to help himself up. He was getting more mobile but still needed his brace for a few more days.

"Are you going to be okay getting there?" I asked. "Not like I don't doubt Keith's strength or anything, but he needs to be careful."

"I'll be fine, but thanks." He wobbled over to his closet. "What time do you need to get ready for college boy?"

I looked at my watch. "I probably should leave soon. Do you think it's strange that he's taking me?"

Levi shook his head. "I would find it odd if anybody *didn't* want to take you anywhere you wanted to go."

I was stunned by Levi's response. It was sweet and exactly what I needed to hear. Usually we're ribbing each other, so I almost didn't know how to respond to such a sincere gesture.

As if Alex could read my mind, he called as I was saying good-bye to Levi. "Better take this," I said as I went into the hallway for some privacy.

"Hey, I'm so glad I caught you," Alex seemed out of breath. "I feel awful."

"Is everything all right?" I asked.

"No, I'm so sorry, but I can't go tonight." I heard shouting in the background. "My friends convinced me to rush, and the frat we're interested in wants us to . . . well, I can't really say, except that I won't be going anywhere this entire weekend."

And here I'd been thinking I'd have to wait a couple years before a frat boy broke my heart.

Although my heart wasn't really broken. I was excited to hang out with Alex, but not as much as I should've been. I knew what it was like to like someone. And I didn't have those feelings for Alex.

"It's okay." I made some other comments to make Alex feel better, when in reality, he should've been comforting me. I don't even remember how we ended the conversation.

But I do remember seeing Levi look at me through a partially opened door.

I gave him a smile. "Well, Alex can't make it. So I'm going to go home and consume a bunch of food and watch a sappy movie, as one does in these circumstances."

Levi looked at me intensely. "Do you want to go with me?"

I shook my head. "I'm not going to be the third wheel."

He hobbled forward. "No, that's not what I'm asking. Macallan, do you want to go to the dance with me?"

He wasn't making sense. "What about Stacey?"

"Can you forget about Stacey and everybody else for a second? I'm asking you a simple question: Do you want to go with me?"

But it wasn't a simple question. Of course, I wanted to go to the dance with Levi. I loved to do anything with Levi. We always had fun together, even when he'd complain about his injury.

Levi took my hand. "Macallan, I just need a yes or a no."

I could feel tears sting the back of my eyes as I denied myself the one thing I truly wanted. I pulled my hand away. "Listen, don't worry about me. I better go. You don't want to keep your group waiting."

I turned my back and rushed down the stairs, knowing he couldn't catch up to me. But as I walked out the front door, I replayed in my head what I wanted to say. What I wished I had the courage to say.

Yes, Levi. I want to go to the dance with you. I want you to put your arms around me. I don't want to pretend that you and I are nothing more. My life is better off with you in it. I want to be with you. Because I love you, Levi. And not just as friends.

Hallelujah! She has seen the light!

I can't even . . .

No, please, allow me.

CHAPTER EIGHTEEN

Knowing Macallan as long as I have allows me some insights into the way she is. For instance, I knew she was freaked out when she ran out of my room that night.

There wasn't much that scared her. She was the strongest person I'd ever known. And I'm not talking about the kind of strength that's measured by the number of reps someone can perform.

I'm talking about being fearless. About standing up for yourself. About not caring what people think.

Yet something was scaring her. There was a reason she bolted and didn't make one of her jokes.

But I couldn't put my finger on it.

Or, more accurately, I didn't want to get my hopes up.

"California!" Keith patted my shoulder during the dance. "Give me warning if you hit the dance floor. You know my moves can't be contained."

"Thanks," I mumbled.

"What's his problem?" he asked Stacey.

She shrugged. I knew I should've acted happy to be there, for her sake. I knew I should've done a lot of things.

As I surveyed the group of friends around me, I thought about how much I'd wanted this when I'd first moved here. A group of friends. To be part of the popular crowd. To be one of the top athletes.

That's what I'd thought I wanted.

But now I knew that what I wanted and what I needed were entirely different.

I didn't have to decide between this life or Macallan. I knew that. But I did have a choice to make: to sit there and pass by something important to me or go to Macallan and tell her how I felt. And make her listen. I knew the risk I was taking. There was a strong possibility that she would leave and spend senior year at the International Space Station.

But she'd paused when I asked her if she wanted to go to the dance. She'd known that wasn't exactly what I was asking. But she hadn't said no. She'd paused, and in the pause I knew that maybe, just maybe, she felt the same way I did.

I had to stop pretending and go after what I wanted. What I needed.

"Stacey," I said lightly. This was going to suck. "I'm really sorry, but I need to go."

She nodded like she was expecting it. "Macallan?"

She knew. *Everybody* knew. All those times people asked us if we were together, or teased us that we acted like an old married couple, it was because everybody saw what we were both too stubborn to see.

I opened my mouth to reply, but couldn't find the right words to say. How could you tell someone you really think she's great but you're in love with someone else?

"It's okay," Stacey said. "I've been expecting this for a while."

"I don't want you to think this has anything to do with you." I felt guiltier with each word.

"I know. I mean, seriously, Levi?" She actually smiled. "We all knew that you'd eventually end up with Macallan. I guess I should be offended, but maybe I read too many romance novels to not want to cheer for the two best friends. And you know, we had fun. You were nice to me." She shrugged.

I guess that showed how much our relationship meant to either of us, that it could be summed up with a shrug of the shoulders.

"I'm going to get back to . . ." She motioned toward her friends on the dance floor. "Good luck."

"Thanks." I was going to need it.

I hobbled to the exit, wishing I could rip the brace off and run to her. The cold February air hit my face as I realized I didn't have a ride to her house. I called her, but she didn't answer her phone. I called the Dietzes' home number and still got no answer. I didn't want to ask my mom or dad to drive me around. It felt almost too personal.

Suddenly, I knew exactly who I could call. The one person who would help me out, no matter what. And do it with a smile on his face.

Adam pulled up less than ten minutes after I called him. He hadn't asked me a bunch of questions. I'd told him I needed a ride and he'd asked where I was.

"Hey, Levi, how you doing?" He popped out of the driver's seat to help me into his car.

"Great. Thanks so much, Adam." He made sure I was all the way in before he slammed the door.

"Do you need to go home?" he asked.

"I really need to talk to Macallan. Do you know if she's home?"

He shook his head, then put the car into drive. "There's only one way to find out."

Mercifully, Adam stayed quiet on the short drive to Macallan's house. We pulled up and noticed that a couple of lights were on in the living room. Adam helped me out of the car and used his keys to let us in.

"Macallan?" he called out. My heart was beating so fast.

No answer.

I tried her phone again and heard it ringing. I followed the noise to the kitchen table, where the phone sat unattended.

Adam joined me in the kitchen. "She's not upstairs. I checked the closet, and her coat's gone. Do you want me to call her dad? He's working late tonight."

"No." The last thing I needed was Mr. Dietz getting a call that Macallan was missing.

Everybody else was at the dance. So it wasn't like she was hanging out with Danielle. Wherever she was, she was by herself. Maybe she needed to get some fresh air and think.

Then it hit me: I knew exactly where she was.

"Adam, can you take me to Riverside Park?"

I couldn't bear being stuck at home by myself while everybody else was at the dance. It wasn't like I'd never spent a Saturday night home alone, but there was something that set my nerves on edge that night.

And that something was Levi.

I needed to clear my head, so I went for a walk. Nothing

helped. I thought I was being random with each turn I took, but then I found myself at Riverside Park.

I sat on the swings and rocked myself back and forth. What I thought would give me comfort made me feel worse. I felt more alone than ever without Levi there to push me.

I always felt a little alone without him near me.

At first I thought my mind was playing tricks on me when I heard his familiar shuffle. I assumed it was my longing for him that had manifested into what I was hearing.

Then I heard his voice.

"Macallan?"

She paused for a second before she slowly turned around.

"Levi? What are you doing here? Why aren't you at the dance? Was that Adam's car that just drove away?"

"Yeah." I know I only answered her last question because I had no idea what to say to her. "Can we talk?"

She helped me to the picnic bench, the same one we'd met at a few months before. We sat down and my body instantly tensed up from the cold.

"I have something I need to tell you," I said, "and I really need you to hear me out before you say anything . . . or run away to Ireland."

I was expecting a snarky comment or a scared look on her face. All she said was "I promise."

At this point, I realized there was no going back.

So I took a deep breath.

"I left the dance because I wasn't with you. You and I both know I've been an idiot these last few months. All along I thought that what I wanted out of my high school life was to be with the guys, to have a girlfriend, to be on a team. But even when I had those things, I didn't feel complete. And that's because I'm not complete without you."

I couldn't take it anymore. "Levi, stop. Please." I knew I'd promised not to say anything, but he needed to hear what I had to say.

"I know," I told him. I looked down at the ground — for some reason, I didn't think I could say everything if I had to look at him. "I know what you're going to say because I feel the same way."

My heart stopped. "You do?"

She finally looked at me. "Of course."

"But what about Ireland?"

She smiled at me. It shattered my heart into a million pieces. "You're not the only one who's done stupid things."

I think my confession of being an idiot left him speechless. I didn't blame him. It wasn't something I copped to often.

"Macallan?" I was terrified. But I knew I would never forgive myself if I didn't give it one more try.

"I love you."

I wasn't going to waste this opportunity again. I wasn't going to be scared. I wasn't going to run away. I wasn't going to make excuses.

I almost couldn't breathe for the few seconds after I spoke. She turned to me and leaned in. I moved forward.

We were only inches away from each other. My entire body pulsated with anticipation. We had kissed before, and not too far from the spot we were in, but this time it was different. It wasn't a joke, it wasn't something I did to shut him up, it was something *we* did because we wanted to.

I kissed her.

I kissed him.

It. Was.

Brilliant.

Unlike the first time we kissed, I was anticipating it. I relished her lips on mine. Her hand gently ran through my hair. I pulled her in closer to me, not wanting to have a distance between us ever again.

Even though it was cold outside, I felt nothing but warmth being next to Levi. He pulled away from me briefly to kiss my forehead. "You have no idea how happy you just made me."

"I think I do," I replied.

We sat there for a few minutes, his lips resting against my forehead. Us leaning on each other, like always.

This did change everything, but I knew that could be a

good thing. Because what we had between us was something I'd never had with anybody else. I couldn't comprehend being as close to another person the way I was with Levi.

I had been resisting this, but I couldn't deny that it felt right.

This was how things should've been for us. I think we both knew that. I felt Macallan shiver slightly. "Let's go home," I said as I gave her another kiss.

Even though I didn't specify which home we'd be going to, it didn't matter. This entire time I'd been thinking about where my home was. At first it was California, then Wisconsin. But in truth, home isn't necessarily where you sleep at night.

It's where you feel like yourself.

Where you're most comfortable.

Where you don't have to pretend, where you can be just you.

I had finally reached that place because Macallan is home to me.

So, as I was saying, guys and girls can be friends.

Best friends.

And what's better than falling in love with your best friend?

Nothing.

You always have to get the last word in, don't you?

You know it.

Yes, I do.

Yep.

Oh, Macallan . . .

Yes, Levi?

I love you.

I love you, too.

And there you are again, having to get the last word in.

But I don't think you mind.

Not at all.

Good.

ACKNOWLEDGMENTS

Blimey if I know where I'd be without David Levithan, the Floyd to my Buggy (that's a compliment — I swear!). I'm so happy you said, "Hey, what about writing a book about a guy and girl who are best friends. . . ." I'm honored to have you as an editor, a friend, musical consigliere, and Target chauffeur.

I'm much better off with the fantastic crew at Scholastic behind me. I know how much work goes into getting a book out into the world, and appreciate all of your efforts. Four scoops of custard to Tracy van Straaten, Bess Braswell, Emily Morrow, Stacy Lellos, Alan Smagler, Leslie Garych, Lizette Serrano, Emily Heddleson, Candace Greene, Antonio Gonzalez, Joy Simpkins, Elizabeth Starr Baer, Sue Flynn, Nikki Mutch, and all the sales reps.

Thanks to my agent, Rosemary Stimola, for sprinting the distance with me time and time again.

I owe so much to my family, especially my parents for enduring the torture that was researching Culver's and Friday night fish fries with me. And my siblings: Eileen,

Meg, and WJ, for always cheering on their baby sis. It means the world to me.

I'm so grateful that I have wonderful friends who also make excellent readers: Rose Brock, Jen Calonita, and Bethany Strout. Your input made this book so much better.

In the words of the Almighty K. Clark, my life would suck without: Chris Miller, who bravely drove on the wrong side of the road during our trip around Ireland; Susan North and Amy Miller, who let me crash at their places when I needed peace and quiet; Mark Dowd, Amy Royce, Justina Chen, and my Facebook friends for answering my questions about ACL surgery; Macallan Durkin, who let me borrow her name. And of course my wonderful author friends who've made what can be a very solitary job into a community of awesome.

I'd be remiss to not acknowledge the brilliant Nora Ephron, who not only gave the world Harry and Sally, but countless other timeless characters and stories. I'll always have what she's having.

To every bookseller, librarian, teacher, and blogger who has recommended my books and every reader who has picked up one of my books: I wouldn't have this job without you. I know every day how lucky I am to have it, and never take it (or you) for granted. THANK YOU!

Elizabeth Eulberg can totally be just friends with certain boys, as long as they have good taste in music. It also helps if the boy is a Green Bay Packers fan. When she's not busy going through potential friends' iPods, she's busy writing about what she finds out from being friends with guys. She's also the author of *The Lonely Hearts Club*, *Prom & Prejudice*, *Take a Bow*, and *Revenge of the Girl with the Great Personality*. You can find her on the web at www.elizabetheulberg.com.

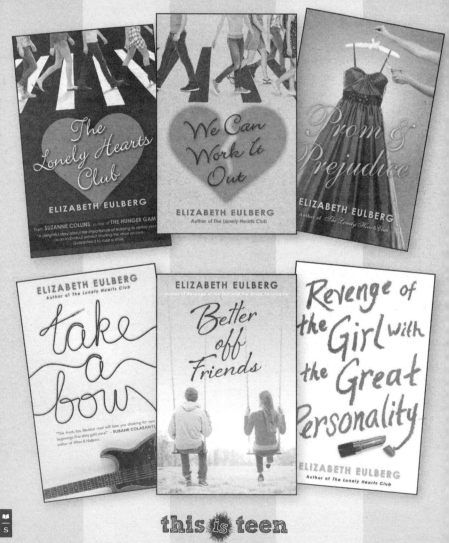

SMART and FUNNY
novels you'll love from
ELIZABETH EULBERG